Consequence

a significance series novella

SHELLY CRANE

SHELLY CRANE
NEW YORK TIMES Bestselling Author

Printed in the USA

1 2 3 4 5 6 7 8 9 10

Available in paperback, Kindle and eBook formats through Amazon, CreateSpace, Barnes & Noble, Apple, Kobo, and anywhere eBooks are sold.

More information can be found at the author's websites:

http://shellycrane.blogspot.com

https://www.facebook.com/shellycranefanpage

https://twitter.com/AuthShellyCrane

One

I peeked into the grand hall toward our room on the first floor. It was one of the things I never fought the council on—to be separated from everyone else. Their Visionary was royalty. Fine. So Caleb and I stayed in the same room for every reunification. The kids stayed in the room next to us until they were old enough to start staying upstairs with everyone else by themselves. They got paired up with cousins of the same sex.

They loved it. It was like sleepovers. Ava was only six now, so it was her first year to sleep upstairs without us. Today was our next to last day. We were going home tomorrow. We had been pretty busy all day. I'd barely seen Caleb. Correction, I had seen Caleb for all of ten minutes. Even after all this time, my body still ached for him. We still went into withdrawals for each other. I looked at the door longingly, not sure if he was in there or not, but wanting to see him so badly.

"Mamma?" I looked down at the little boy tugging on my dress.

"Rodney? What are you doing down here?" I hoisted him to my hip.

"Visionary?" Paulo called from the table. No matter how hard he tried, Paulo was a good man, but a serial flip-flopper. He would be totally on board with change one year, then right back to tradition the next season. One little wrench in the cog and he was done. He couldn't understand that when you changed things, you were going to have bumps in the road. It was inevitable.

I smiled in allowance. "Coming, councilor."

Our last day luncheon was almost underway and then we'd be on our way home. I walked with Rodney to the table and looked over the proposition. The councilman on the end was asleep, his head leaned back on the chair with his mouth open slightly. He was dreaming about Christmas morning with his grandkids. They opened the train whistles that he handmade, whittled by his hands, and drove the entire house crazy with whistle sounds. But he was so proud.

Rodney tugged on the ends of my hair. "Do it, Mommy." He giggled before I'd even had a chance to do anything, the image of what he wanted playing through his mind. "Do it, please," he begged in a high-pitched whisper.

I smiled down at him and leaned in conspiratorially. We looked at the councilman as I flicked my finger up. The man's hair piece lifted from the front of his head just a little. I let it fall and then lifted it again. Rodney giggled so hard into his hands as I continued to dislodge the poor man's toupee a few more times really fast.

"Visionary," Paulo said wryly. I cut my eyes to him and smiled crookedly, a silent question there. "Are you…finished? If we sign these papers, we can be on our way, and the luncheon can begin."

"We're almost done," I spouted back regally and went back to show Rodney once more. "Ok. We're done now. Go find Daddy, sport."

"Right here. That didn't take long, did it?" I heard from behind me right before warm hands crashed into my hips. His mouth moved to my ear and my lips parted as his calm shot through my veins as he whispered, "I couldn't stand it another second without you."

Even in the room with other people, I leaned back into his arms. "Caleb," I said thankfully.

"Councilors, are we about done here?" he asked, and anyone could tell he was beyond peeved at the way this trip had turned out. We'd hardly gotten to see each other at all. They'd been particularly greedy of my time. That's what I was there for, I knew, but this had been one of those trips where the rules had outweighed the fun. They worried far too much about everything and instead of just leaving things up to my visions and the future, they insisted on the old ways of doing things. They were beginning to let their fear sway them again and not believe in the Visionary. So the entire week was spent in meetings and debate instead of revelry and splendor as it should have been.

"Now, Caleb," Paulo began, and I heard Caleb's answer before it came. I winced.

"You've kept her cooped up in here, and Gran, too, for that matter, all week. A Visionary on the verge of withdrawals because she's working too hard and long doesn't sound like a Visionary that's able to perform at the best of her abilities."

One of them sputtered, "She's doing just fine. Perfectly adequate."

Caleb chuckled. "I have no doubt that she's adequate, councilor, but think of how great she could be if you'd let her be fully energized instead of keeping her constantly on a short leash. All of you." He took my hand and stood next to me, his shoulder brushing mine. "I get it. You want to look brave, set an example and be leaders for our people. You think that anything but diplomacy and matters of business and politics makes you look weak. But the very foundation of our people was built on the bond between two people. I think embracing that would benefit our people way greater than trying to fight it for some show of wills."

Paulo turned his ring on his finger. He missed his wife and constantly thought about her. They talked in his mind all the time. He had to know I heard them, but didn't care or knew that I was a sap to my core and wouldn't mind it. He wasn't brave though. No matter what he wanted for himself, he always went with the flow.

Always. And the flow of the council usually went with whatever seemed the hardest. Without waiting for whatever they were going to say, Caleb put his arm around my waist and started to pull me from the room. "No offense, gentleman, but you've kept her from me long enough. Go spend the last day with your families before everyone goes home."

Gran came and took Rodney's hand quickly. "I've got him." She grinned haughtily. "And I've got Ava, too. Go on, pretty girl."

"Thanks, Gran," Caleb told her, throwing a grateful smile over his shoulder for her. We picked up the pace as we heard the minds of the council begin to stop being so flabbergasted and start to think of something to say to stop us.

We sprinted through the hall like teenagers and I found myself giggling, especially when we reached the stairwell to find Kyle and Lynne were there, too. Kyle smirked at my surprised face. "Oh, come on. Do you really think the Champion would be able to pull off a ruse like that without some help?"

I ignored him with a smile and looked up at my significant. "Where are we going?"

"Does it even matter?" he said lovingly and leaned down to kiss my forehead, resting his lips there. "Just don't ever stop touching me," he whispered.

"It really is stupid," Kyle muttered and looked at the air around us. The blue ribbons no longer just danced around us, they crackled. The power between us had gotten stronger over the years. Between me as the Visionary and him as the Champion, and the fact that they insisted on working us to the bone when we were here, when we finally did get together, it was like fireworks. If you got sympathy from Kyle, you knew it was bad. "They're just torturing themselves. I don't get it."

"Paulo thinks of nothing but his wife the whole time," I mused. "His mind isn't on what we're talking about. He's the worst one of all, yet he seems to be the worst flip-flopper." I leaned back. "I've searched their minds for some reason behind it. It seems almost like there was something else going on, but…I can't see anything."

"But if it was in regards to you, you wouldn't see it, right? Your visions?" Lynne asked. She had kept the blond hair, but let it grow to an insane length, almost down to her butt. Kyle was infatuated with it. I was constantly tuning him out. His hands were always playing with it, twirling his fingers around the golden strands. But then there were *other* things he did with it, too, and I didn't want to be privy to that.

"No," I shook my head, "but whatever. Let's go. No more talk of councils. You snuck me away," I reached up and bit into Caleb's bottom lip, "so let's not waste time."

He groaned in his mind where no one would hear him but me. *Why the hell did I invite Kyle? I'd much rather have you alone right now.*

There will be plenty of time for that, gorgeous.

I smiled as I threw one of the lines he used to always say to me back at him. He rolled his eyes playfully and growled a laugh.

"You're impossible, Visionary." He turned me and put his hands on my hips, guiding me to walk in front of him as we made our way up the stairs. He was enjoying the view. He always let me go first. I smiled and took the ends of my hair in my fingers—my hair that had grown back long ago and was way past my shoulders now. I had to say that Caleb loved my long hair, too.

Once we reached the roof of the palace, I realized that it had been two reunifications since I'd been up there, this would have been my third. The last two, I hadn't had time, been too busy, too much drama.

Gah…it was so beautiful.

A warm hand tugged on mine and I looked at his insistent face with an irked raised brow. He grinned, a little sheepish. "I know you're enjoying the view, baby, but we're losing daylight."

We walked over the rooftops and over to the greenhouse. Or where it used to be, rather, where Donald's "statue" had once stood. The council let the family take his body home. They said it was disrespectful to leave him up there, even if he had tried to plot and ruin our people and legacies, even if he had tried to kill Caleb and me. I shook my head as I looked at that spot and remembered it all as if it were yesterday.

Caleb reached over the edge and grabbed the rope. We took the brand new lift down toward the bottom and now, I could enjoy my view. Kyle knew we needed this ride right now and took the rope without even being asked, being the one to lower us to the bottom.

Caleb's head rested on my shoulder as his arms gathered me as close as I could get, smashed into his chest in a warm cocoon. He would look out at the buildings that looked so amazing as the sun sat atop the city in the noon haze, but mostly he was completely and utterly consumed with me. His soft lips rubbed the skin of my neck, making his rough chin rub it in turn, the contrast heating me all over.

Pretty soon, I could no longer take it. I leaned my head back and to the side to accept his lips on mine just as we banged to the bottom. He sighed, his tongue licking his lip, and licking mine in the process. "Daggumit," he growled. "Everything is always keeping you from me."

I smiled crookedly and turned to walk backward from the lift, taking his hand. "Come on, Jacobson."

Lynne and Kyle walked in front of us, holding hands and talking in their minds about their son's birthday party. He wanted a miniature pony to go along with the horse that Kyle bought for Lynne. They had a house outside of town - a ranch really. In the summer, we took some of the kids from our tutoring program out there and they did some riding lessons and camping trips.

It was so much fun to watch the kids' faces light up. Some of them had never seen a horse up close before.

"Where are we going?" I asked distractedly as I stared up at the sun coming over the treetops.

Thirty-six percent of ninety is thirty-two point four.

I laughed. "Oh, my gosh, Jacobson. What have you done?"

He smirked his signature smirk and leaned in close. "Stop poking around and just enjoy the ride."

He kissed my temple, and with linked our fingers he put his arm around my shoulder to pull me close.

We passed a fountain on the square as we crossed the street. It was beautiful, and I found myself staring at it as Caleb tugged me along the cobblestone road.

And then a scream blared through my mind.

I knew it wasn't real. I knew it. But I still found myself gasping and seizing Caleb's shirt in my fists. He heard the scream through me and gripped my upper arms as it descended through the air, almost as if it were coming closer.

"Maggie!" he pleaded in a hiss and shook me slightly. "A vision?"

But no vision came. I heard a splash to my right and jerked my gaze to follow the sound, but saw nothing but calm water in the fountain across the street. The scream was gone. Caleb's hands pulled my face up and he still looked like that boy that would move mountains and break jaws for me. "Baby?"

"It wasn't a vision, or at least I don't think so. It's happening again," I finally answered, my eyes on his chin. I let my eyes drift to his. He was worried, yes, but angry that his plan for our day was about to be ruined. It seemed they were ruined a lot lately. There were strange things happening all the time over the past couple of weeks—interrupting my dreams, strange flashes of visions that weren't really visions at all. I shook my head. "No, it wasn't a vision."

He sighed forcefully, his thumb sweeping over my cheekbone and down my neck, his calm slamming into my veins like a shot. "Hell, Maggie," he groaned and it pained me to hear the agony in his voice. "I feel so useless. I don't know what to do for you—"

"This is because I'm the Visionary," I insisted. "It has to be, Caleb. There's no other logical reason. It's my burden—"

He leaned back enough to see my face, his own face fierce and the protectiveness all over him. "Your burdens are mine. Don't you ever forget that—Visionary or not."

I heard Kyle and Lynne off to the side. They could see something was going on and were giving us space to work it out. It gave Caleb an idea. He whipped his angry gaze back to scowl at Lynne. "Did you do that to the water? Kyle, are y'all playing around?"

"No," Kyle answered for her easily. "Why?"

"Because you're always playing around," Caleb muttered and looked back at me. "Something's going on. Something bigger than just Visionary duties. All the nightmares you've been having, all the times your visions have come but nothing came with it, just a sound or a flash, and I couldn't see it with you. It's not normal. We have to figure out what's going on—take this to the council."

I glanced at the fountain and back to him. His worries were practically tied in knots, right there between us, as his palms rubbed warm circles into the skin of my forearms, trying anything and everything to get his calm to seep in.

I took a deep breath and held it for a few long seconds. "No. No council. Look," I smiled as best I could, "let's just have the day you planned for us, okay? I promise I'll look into it and we'll do some digging before we go home. We will figure this out. There's got to be a reason, there always is, and I'll find it."

Ashlyn…the previous Visionary. Maybe she had something to say about this.

He chewed on his lip and sighed through his nose. "Baby," he complained in a low voice. "I hate this."

"I know."

He sucked his lip into his mouth, which let me know he was really thinking about it. He was remembering the first time he saw me at the stoplight. How he knew that I was going to be his that day, and he'd do anything and everything to make sure that I was safe and sound and happy.

"You're not failing at any of it," I assured him and leaned up on my toes. I draped my arms over his shoulders and pressed my nose to his, just like he used to do to me. "Now if you'll feed me, I'll be completely fulfilled."

He managed a small chuckle at my joke, but I knew it was just for my benefit. He pulled me up the rest of the way to meet his lips and the gruff display did nothing to reassure me that he was actually fine.

I let it slide.

Linking our fingers, we joined Kyle and Lynne again who seemed way too worried for my liking. When Kyle's mind floated his thoughts back and forth, worrying about his Visionary, I knew he'd crossed sides and was now a traitor—no longer my friend who worked beside me and called me Maggie, but had reverted back to a Virtuoso member who was in reverent awe of his Visionary. And right now—worried sick.

"I'm fine," I assured them all. "Don't make me pull rank on y'all. We're going to have a great day with no kids and no council and no gnats, right? Come on."

Caleb sighed and looked over at them. His grip tightened on my fingers, but they didn't say anything. He gave me a smile. One of those dimple smiles that I loved so much. I guess they figured they'd rather stay silent than lie.

I knew they worried about the Visionary. I knew I was more than just a person. I was a symbol. The Visionary was important. That was the real reason they were freaked. Who knew when the next one would come again, and I hadn't gotten half of the things done I wanted—

"Don't."

I looked over to see Caleb's smile long gone. "What?"

"How could you say that?" he asked, the hurt in his eyes was so evident, it stung my own to feel it through him. "After everything, after all these years and everything we've been through, you still think I look at you as the Visionary first?"

Two

My breath eased out slowly. I had hurt him.

"Don't you know?" Lynne asked and flicked her nosy eyes between us. "You're in each other's minds all day and night."

"We leave a few stones unturned," Caleb answered gruffly. "We like to leave some mystery. We like to talk about things instead of just always knowing everything."

She glared at Kyle—just a small flick of her eyes. "This big dork won't stay out of my head."

Kyle ignored her and squinted at Caleb, shaking his head a little. "You don't see her as the Visionary first? Really?"

"She's my significant first," Caleb said harder.

I was a little surprised by it. No, I hadn't really thought much about it. I had always assumed the two things were neck and neck but Visionary was probably winning. He had just stolen me from a meeting though, hadn't he?

"But you weren't that way in California," Kyle reminded him. "When we found out who she was in the beginning, you were just as obsessed about it as I—"

"And I paid for acting like an ass, if you remember," Caleb told him. He sighed as his blue eyes found mine and he remembered how he watched me leave in the Jeep that night, feeling my heart beating so loud in his chest, and not knowing what was going to happen next. Knowing he'd screwed up, but not knowing what to do to fix it.

I shook my head and opened my mouth to tell him no, that I was sorry, but Kyle beat me to it.

"She'll always be the Visionary, no matter what you want. Or what she wants." He crossed his arms and scowled at us both. "Maybe that's what's going on right now. That you both are taking the Visionary thing too lightly and it's pissed off, trying to send you a message—"

Caleb moved before I could stop him. He got right in Kyle's face, nose to nose, and growled, "You don't live it and breathe it every day. You have no idea what you're talking about."

Kyle scoffed, but had the good sense to back down enough to show he wasn't about to go head to head with the Champion of his clan. "I'm not trying to fight with you. I'm just stating fact…" Caleb moved forward and Kyle changed his wording,

"I'm just talking ideas. There's a reason this is happening to Maggie."

I gripped Caleb's arm—not to hold him back, but to just hold him. "Don't ever say that Maggie hasn't done enough or given enough or not taken being the Visionary seriously. She was yanked into this life by me and has done nothing but accept and love us, all of us. So shut your face with talk that she's not absolutely amazing at what she's been given and had to deal and work with. Even the ones of us that grew up in it wouldn't do so well."

Kyle sighed and raised his hands. "I didn't mean for it to come out like that." He glanced at me and back at Caleb. "Both of you work hard. I just mean that maybe you're spreading yourselves thin. Or…maybe focusing on the wrong things. Maybe you're not on the right path and this is a little course correction from the universe. It's obvious that Maggie's not doing something right or this wouldn't be happening, right?"

Caleb's hands snapped forward and gripped Kyle's collar tightly.

"Caleb!" Lynne screeched from Kyle's back.

"Champion or not," Caleb growled, "I will bust you in your mouth if you don't stop talking about my wife that way."

"See!" Kyle said and pointed above Caleb's hands. "You said 'my wife', not 'her', not 'Maggie', not 'the Visionary'.

You're looking at this all wrong, bro." He shook his head and pushed Caleb's hands off. "If it were me—"

"If it were you, you'd be even worse than I am," Caleb said, the fight completely gone out of him. He sagged, his head leaning down to rest his chin to his chest. I still had his arm in my grip, just watching the display.

"Maybe," Kyle conceded.

You would. You know you would.

I ignored Lynne's internal scold to Kyle and put my hand on Caleb's scruffy chin to pull his face over to me. I pushed everything away but him and me. I moved and pressed right up against him, his chest and thigh to mine, letting my nose and cheek rest against his—our own little secret place, he called it. With our eyes closed, I tried to think of a way to apologize to the man I loved more than life. He was right. He had thought of me as a woman first, as his wife, as Maggie, first. That's what I'd always wanted and took it for granted, thinking it had always been the opposite.

Our lives were busy, absolutely, between Champion and Visionary business, the family, the kids and the centers, but we made it work. And it worked perfectly, it seemed. It felt like our balance was pretty spot-on.

Except for the week of the reunification. We barely saw each other while everyone else was busy having fun with their games and family and friend time. I barely got to catch up with anyone, and my significant and I were on the border of withdrawals the entire time.

I'd studied the photos that Rodney had taken of the previous Visionary, Ashlyn's, scribed wall over the years. I did everything I was supposed to do, in my gut. I followed my gift, my ability, which was given to me to help change this race of people. I knew it wasn't going to be instant, but had to be done. I saw that in my vision. I knew it was going to be hard sometimes. I didn't know how else I could follow my path. I was doing everything I could.

And Caleb. My sweet Caleb. He was always carrying the torch for me. Even now, ready to bust up Kyle for bad mouthing me when I didn't even have faith enough to know what was in my own husband's head.

His hands came up, finally caving, as he cupped my face. He shook his head.

Do you know how long it's been since I've been in that beautiful head of yours?

Too long.

I mean it. Any idea how long since we've been able to really talk like this without a room full of council members taking your attention? Or exhaustion claiming us at the end of the night? Or kids asking us to put them in bed? Or since I've gotten to be in your mind at all for anything? Four days. Four days, Maggie. That's an eternity for our kind. Do you know how long it's been since we've mutualized?

Six days. I've been counting.

That's not okay. It's not your fault at all. I'm just saying, how can we be expected to be in sync and be the couple we're supposed to be if the basic tools we were given aren't even being allowed to us? If you're taken from me the second you get here, then how are you supposed to know what's going on with me? And I you? They've made us weak like this—all of the council couples.

I should have made the effort. I should have paid attention. I rubbed his nose a little with mine so he'd know that this point was more important than the rest. *I should have known better. I should have known what was in your head without even having to look. I just...the Visionary is always so front and center for everyone, especially here. I just let my assumptions lump you into that, too. I'm really sorry, baby.*

His hands moved, caressing down my arms and back, all the way down to wrap against my lower back. He sighed into my neck as he lifted me, pressing me against him. *Gah, sweetheart. Do you have any idea how much I've missed you? My imprint has been going absolutely insane needing to be with you and to just...*

Say it.

Consume every inch and piece of you.

I gripped him tighter. *Mine, too. I'm sorry.*

Before he could say anything, I slammed past his barriers, one after another. He groaned against my mouth, a small noise only for me, and held me tighter as I refused to let anything keep him from me a second longer. His protective barrier was there, ever ready, ever present and beautiful in his love for me.

Our memories had changed over the years. We had kids and our lives were vastly different, but so much the same. Now in his loop of visions I saw, my aching and laboring over our daughter's birth was there…the look on my face as I held her in my arms for the first time and then looked at him with such thanks for giving me such a gift…him watching me over the years as I did all I could for our people. The council may not like me very much, but even I had to admit that our people were a different story. As soon as the imprints started coming back, they realized that things were turning around and there was a shift in the balance. Even though I had fought it back then, I had been that balance. They were grateful and the more I embraced it, the closer I got to the people. I didn't get to spend much time with them at reunifications, but I talked to them a lot from home during the year. The first year alone we had sixteen couples imprint of all ages.

People like Haddock, who were older and thought they'd never imprint, were now doing so, finally getting the life they'd always been promised. But it wasn't everyone. It wasn't all the older people who hadn't imprinted when they were younger, and people questioned why. I knew it had to do with our intentions, our actions, our progress as a race. I explained that. I explained that our life, our gifts and abilities, were just that—gifts. Those could be taken at any moment just like before, and we needed to remember that what we are is a privilege and honor, not a right.

Past all that, past the linings of his mind was our life and the sweet things of inconsequence that piled up, but still made me ache with its sweetness. His kids from the centers he loved so much were in there, his family, his guitar—still his favorite instrument, and he played all the time—but at the core of him, right at the heated center, there was nothing there but me.

Us.

I could feel Caleb's arms binding around me tighter still as he picked me up before cold bricks met my back. In his mind, I saw he'd moved us out of the middle of the street and into a small alley between the bakery and the deli. Kyle and Lynne were long gone somewhere.

Don't think about them, or where we are, or what's going to happen. Just me. Only me.

I obeyed him as if his voice was pushing the buttons that controlled my very being. He caged me in, one arm around my neck and one around my lower back. When his mind eased back inside mine, he was walking the ledge of control. And so was I.

It had been a very long time since I'd lost control and not been able to rein in my ability, but when I saw a blue ribbon crackle behind my eyelid, I gasped into his mouth.

Hold on, baby. Just hold on. You need this just as much as I do.

More. I gripped his brown curls and pulled his mouth down to mine. *I'm so close to losing it.*

It's their fault, he growled even as he devoured my tongue with his. He dove deep and used his hips to pin me to the bricks. *They've got to stop treating you like an object and remember that you're just like them.*

No more, I begged. *No more talk of them. Just kiss me until I can't think of anything at all.*

He caved and not another word was spoken. His love and respect for my wishes was given in his answer to my request. He always did anything and everything to give me what I wanted. If there was a problem that he couldn't solve, it wasn't just his own upset, it was a physical need to see it through that hurt him. That's why all this stuff with the council didn't make anything easy. And it didn't make much sense either.

Why were they so hell bent on making things so hard?

But as Caleb picked me up in his arms, my knees on the side of his hips, and carried me a little bit farther into the alley, I was done worrying about it.

As the building touched my back this time, I saw he'd moved us behind a little outdoor café that wasn't open yet. Must have been only open at night…and it was getting darker.

The fire that sparked between us hadn't dwindled over the years. If anything, it had gotten more intense—more focused, I should say. Centered. Our imprints knew what they wanted and they went for it. No more bumbling around in our insecurity and immaturity. Those days were long gone.

I held my muscles tight, keeping them coiled and sprung for the ready. This was how I kept myself in check, keeping the energy ribbons from popping out everywhere in the air and scaring everyone within a quarter-mile radius.

He pulled my tightly wound leg up, hooking his palm under my thigh, and used his free hand to smooth down my neck to my chest and back up, rubbing his skin into mine. As he tormented me with his big hands, he plundered in my mind, and I gripped my arms around his neck as I felt the first spark zing into my veins. I gasped and opened my mouth to moan or groan or…something, but he swallowed it down and pushed his mind harder, making me his again.

Always mine, his insistent growl reminded me.

As it built, I clung harder and tried to keep myself in check. I hated it. I wanted to cut loose and be myself. At home, we had no worries, but right now, this was about more than just a good time; this was about necessity, a need ingrained in our veins and blood that ached, but still keeping people from seeing my ability at the same time.

I leaned my chin down and squeezed my eyes shut, but he took my chin between his fingers and pulled it back up. He covered my mouth with his, and though he didn't say anything, he didn't have to—he pressed against me, head to toe, and commanded my body to surrender. It was amazing how it worked like that. I shook against his hold, but kept kissing him as our sighs collided between our breaths. The bursts I saw behind my eyelids weren't energy ribbons this time but the mutualizing coming to an end. I gripped his hair tightly in my fingers and found him doing the same thing to the ends of my hair right under my ear—a handful in his fist absentmindedly. The hot and cold zings consumed me, littering my veins until it was all too much. I didn't know how many times we'd mutualized over the years, a million it could've been, but it didn't matter—the first time, the last time, they all were the same and different in their own way, but equally amazing.

He wasn't able to keep the reins as tight on himself like I was and the groan that moved from his lips to my sensitized skin caused goose bumps to run over me. I covered his lips with my fingers and silently begged him to stop before I blew the place up as he moved his hand in his mind to caress my leg, ankle to hip bone.

He chuckled, loving his torture of me as the oblivious passerby's moved in the light just feet away from us. He pulled my wrist up, his panting breaths beating against my skin as he kissed my tattoo with his name lovingly written there. He started to ease away from me, but I gripped his shirt front in my fist. "Not yet. Stay."

"Not going anywhere," he assured as he lifted me and took us to sit in one of the outside deli chairs.

He sat and held me on his lap, but I didn't snuggle in and cuddle. I stared at him. His face, holding a few years more on it, was still hard and gorgeous, his chin strong and his dimples even more defined with his stubble in full force. He was even more handsome with his young, boyish looks on the way out, making room for a very grown-up, powerful looking Champion of our clan. Handsome and loving husband to me, and still being the playful father to my children.

It felt like an eternity had passed sometimes since our wedding, but it had only been ten years in actuality. Still, ten years was a lot to wrap your head around. All those years of letting him love me and trying my best to love him back even more, in return.

I palmed his cheek and rubbed my thumb over his dimple when they made an appearance with his grin. His hands on my sides flexed and caressed up and down my torso as he watched me watch him.

"It's amazing to me that you're still surprised by it," he mused, one of his hands drifting to my neck—to my Visionary mark. He brushed his thumb across it several times before leaning in and kissing it, staying close to me to speak, answering my silent question. "That I love you and this is really our life."

I leaned to the side, gripping his head and sighing into his hair. "It's a good life. It's not uncommon to be grateful to the point of disbelief."

A flash of the visions I had played in the back of my mind and I couldn't help but let it seep into our perfect moment. He wrapped an arm around my lower back and pulled me to him, pressing his face against mine. "I will fix this for you, baby. I will make all the bad things go away. I promise you." I nodded slightly, but he shook his head. "Believe me when I say that whoever is behind this will regret the day they made you suffer."

I leaned back just enough to see his eyes—his honest blue eyes that never lied to me. "You think someone did this on purpose? Not something supernatural?"

He sighed. "This isn't your ability, sweetheart. If it was, then I would see the visions, too. I'd have them with you like I always do. This is something else. It just doesn't feel right. It feels…" he rubbed my upper arms to soothe me as he said the words, "evil."

"The Watsons," my mouth spouted immediately, almost as if the words weren't my own. The Watsons were always the first people who came to mind when I thought of anything that came against us that had evil intentions.

“I can’t prove it, obviously, and I have no real reason to think that. They’d be stupid to show up now after all this time, with no powers and no way to defend themselves. But I feel like they have something to do with it for some reason, like they’ve been waiting in the shadows for the right time to strike.”

He was right. His words rang true in my ears and my veins, but I still felt like I needed to rebel. “Please, no,” I begged in a whisper. “Anything but that.”

Three

"Right now," he said, taking my face in his hands, "I'm taking you for a quiet lunch and we're not going to think about that." He kissed the corner of my mouth and helped me stand.

I stalled and rubbed my palms over the tattoos on his forearms. They were new, one on each arm for each of our kiddos. Rodney's name was on a cog wheel on Caleb's left arm, and Ava's was across a piece of filigree fence with a vine crawling over it. The man carried his whole life on his skin.

Taking my hand, he towed me into the street and ducked into the deli. I knew he could hear Kyle's thoughts as he borrowed my ability. He and Lynne were in the deli already and were waiting for us. They knew we'd come when we were…finished. They knew we'd hear their thoughts and know where they were. Kyle was sorry for being an ass, but still believed that Caleb was wrong for looking at me as the Visionary second. He was a true Ace in his thinking. They all thought that way. He would never understand.

"Maggie is my business," Caleb told him as he pulled my chair out for me, "so let's stop talking about it since we're not going to agree. We don't *have to* agree; that's the beauty of it. She doesn't belong to you."

Kyle rolled his eyes, but lifted his hand as Caleb sat down across from him. "All right, all right. I give, Champion."

"You know I hate it when you call me that," Caleb grumbled and told the waiter he'd have water.

"I know," Kyle rebutted and looked over at me. "Any idea what's going on?"

"No Visionary talk," Caleb ordered. "Maggie has been through enough this week." His hand inched over to mine on the table, his thumb rubbing my knuckles. "We'll figure it out, we always do, but right now we're going to enjoy this last day in London before we go home."

"I think there's probably more important things."

Caleb kept going. "And let Maggie have a few minutes of calm before we go back, because when we do, we've got to figure out who on the council is trying to sabotage us. Because someone is working with the Watsons. We're almost sure of it."

Kyle looked at me and scoffed. "You agree with this bologna?"

I nodded. "Every word."

He gulped. "Whatever you say, boss. I'm right behind you, always."

I told Caleb to order for me. It was our thing. He always ordered for me when we went somewhere new. He knew me inside out and knew what I liked, but today, my mind could barely focus on the glass of water in front of me, let alone what kind of food I wanted. My mind churned with possibilities of who could be behind things and what purpose it could serve.

Stop it, he ordered softly. *Don't make me pull rank.*

I outrank you, Jacobson.

Technically. He grinned, his dimples winking. *I'm still your Champion, however, and I order you to stop worrying until we have to. Whatever this is...we'll deal with it, together.*

Okay. I nodded and sighed, cracking my neck side to side. *I'll try to have fun.*

That's my girl.

The waitress interrupted our flirting with our food of real shepherd's pie, and Kyle and Lynne's kippers. After we ate ourselves full, we walked down Market Street to the shops and marketplace.

The tingling started in the back of my mind softly, like a reminder, but Caleb seemed oblivious to it, so I tried not to think about it at all. I was going to give Caleb the perfect day he wanted if I got nothing else done on this trip.

After a few hours, we finally made our way back toward the lift and I was sporting a new charm for my bracelet—an infinity charm Caleb found. We got Ava and Rodney some things, too, my husband's arms loaded down, making him very cute.

We passed the fountain across the street, the one that I had heard the splash from and seen the vision. I walked cautiously over, half expecting it to be filled with something other than water, but it was crystal clear.

The fountain was beautiful, old in its design and architecture. The woman who sat on top covering herself with a stone blanket smirked at us from her perch. I wondered who she was modeled from, who she was supposed to be. I let the tips of my fingers float across the water, and the vision hit me like no other vision had ever come.

I was falling. It was me, actually me. I wasn't watching them fall. The scream screeched from her lungs—my lungs. I watched the ground come closer and closer, knowing the end was coming, my time was almost over. The fountain was below me like a mirror, portraying an eerie copy of myself and my death.

Right as I braced myself for impact, I was on the roof. I was someone else. I was taller, broader. I couldn't move, but was moving. People moved and talked around me. I was conscience, aware, but not able to interact. They stood me upright when we got to the lift and I saw one of the Watson clan members. I gasped inside my head, but nothing came out of my mouth.

We moved too fast, too swift and with purpose for it to be anything but a plan. I felt a grimy substance all over my thoughts, just like the times I had been in Marcus' and Sikes' heads. What was going on? I reached my mind out, feeling for anything that would bring me some sense of understanding. My own powers no longer worked. I was useless. *No*. I shook that thought away and focused. This was happening for a reason. This was meant for me to see.

When we reached the bottom, we passed the fountain. That fountain… The scream sounded again, but this time, they all heard it. They covered their ears, letting me tumble to the ground. I fell with an awkward thud, like I was stone, molded and unyielding. "It happens sometimes when we come past here," one of them remarked. "Marla's last mark on this world replayed over and over in the fountain's water."

"How come the humans can't hear it?"

"We didn't save her. It's meant to torture us. Only her family can hear it."

That one statement was a dagger to my very soul. *Only her family can hear it…*

I could hear it.

My mother's betrayal was coming back to haunt me yet again.

We were moving. They shoved me in the back of a truck, and in the blink of an eye we were in a house. It was a beautiful place. Clean, bright. They stood me upright in a corner with a room full of people looking at me as if I were the key to all their problems.

"Well, how do we get him out of there?" a woman said.

A man stepped forward. I recognized him from the reunification. His name was Chase.

Chase Watson.

"We don't. He's the only one who could do this; he's the only one who can get himself out. He's stuck like this. He'll make a nice conversation piece right here in the corner for all of eternity." He turned to look at his family. "While we figure out how to avenge him and all our other family in these pathetic human bodies, given to us by the one who was supposed to bring our people more power, not take it away."

Oh, my… I was in Donald's body.

As soon as the thought entered my mind, I was yanked from him and was running in someone else. My feet moved without thought and my eyes wandered around the woods as if looking for someone. I was so tired, I didn't know if I could keep going. I reached the edge of the trees and saw a building. I sprinted for it. My body ached. When I looked down, I saw my belly was bulging and pregnant. I was very close to giving birth. I gasped and cried out, my mind aching, unable to release my own voice and thoughts.

I heard voices behind me and took off again…but didn't get far. They gave chase and soon caught up to me. My mouth spouted words that weren't my own. I listened to them as the men surrounded me and was horrified—beyond horrified—at what I heard.

"Please don't take me back there. Please. I'll do anything you want. Anything. You can have your way with me." My knees hit the dirt as I begged. "I'll do anything! Please, just let the baby and me go! Please!"

"You know that's not going to happen." The one speaking looked down at me without pity or emotion, like I was a job. Like I was something he was supposed to do and nothing else. "You know you're going to have to come back. Just come back the easy way, Gabrielle. You know we don't want to hurt you."

"But you do," I whispered. "You do. And you let him hurt me."

"We want to help you. He wants to make you powerful and help you so that husband of yours can never hurt you again."

I felt my mouth sneer. "He just beat me. Even he never poisoned and tortured me the way you and your family do. You're doing the things you do for you, not me. Don't make it sound like you're helping anyone but yourselves."

He didn't smile. I recognized several of them from the reunification from the Watson family, and I could tell from the clothes they were wearing that this was recent. He pointed his hand toward the truck we all could hear coming in the distance. "Get in the truck, Gabrielle. No one wants to deliver a baby in the woods. He's coming, isn't he?"

A sob escaped my chest and I rose to go with them. I fought inside myself. Me— myself—I wanted to fight. I didn't want them to have this baby. This woman, Gabrielle, she was weak from what they'd put her through. She was just…done. But me, I was ready for a fight. I knew what going with them meant. I knew what Sikes and his family had done to people in the past and apparently his family was carrying the torch in his stead.

Well, I wasn't about to let that happen. I had to do something. There had to be a reason I was seeing this. I focused, I made myself look around and see everything, but Gabrielle climbed into the front seat of the truck, followed by the guy who kept giving orders, and slouched, leaning her head back, giving up. They drove her all the way back to the Watson compound and he took her arm, albeit gently, as he pulled her from the truck and took her back toward the house. "You're going to change things for us, Gabrielle—you and this baby. Doesn't that make you happy? You're finally a part of a family."

"I know you're going to just get rid of me after he's born," Gabrielle whispered.

He didn't say anything back to her, which was answer enough.

Right as I would have breached the threshold of the door, I was slammed back into my own body so forcefully that it felt as if I fell from the sky and had to be caught.

Caleb's arms squeezed me to his chest and his breaths beat against my ear…like he had been breathing hard for a long time. We were both shaking, but Caleb's rage and worry was almost out of control. He was borrowing my ability and *he* was about to lose control and let loose the energy ribbons.

I leaned back, the significant in me forgetting the vision for a second and worry for my Caleb taking over. I was on his lap as he sat on the fountain edge. We were both soaking wet. Nothing made sense, but neither of us said a word as he took my face in his hands and brought my mouth down to his. For once in a really long time, I didn't have to push anything out of my mind. I knew Kyle and Lynne were behind us and probably freaking, but my body was completely, solely, focused on my significant.

It had been a long time since I had been able to do that. I was always so consumed with my Visionary duties since it's this huge part of me. But this was freeing. Even though the vision I just had was so potent, all it did was remind me why this part of my life was that much more important than anything else.

His calm crashed into my veins the same time as his upset did, begging for me to take it away and tell him that I was okay. I pulled his shirt up and pressed my palms flat to his stomach to give him as much of me as I could. His breath faltered against my lips a little and I knew I had made a dent in his thinly controlled concern. His thumbs swept over my cheeks, over and over, reassuring himself that I was still there every time he made a pass.

He didn't wait for me to explain. He sensed it had been traumatic for me anyway, so he just went straight into my mind to find out what happened for himself. He pulled away from my lips and laid his forehead to mine, watching the scenes play out. I hated to watch them all over again, but it was better than trying to explain it. I kept myself in check so there were no energy ribbons. When he finished, he leaned back and finally opened his eyes. He was wrecked. His shaggy, wet hair was flat, wrapping around his ears even when wet.

"You were gone for almost half an hour," he rasped. "I couldn't reach you no matter what I did. Your eyes were closed. It was like you were asleep. I couldn't see what you were seeing, your vision. You never said a word, never moved, barely breathed."

"Why am I wet?"

"You touched the water—the fountain took you under." I squinted in confusion. "It sucked you in. I jumped in after you."

I sighed. "The Watsons…they're not finished with us."

"What the hell does all this mean?" he growled and smoothed my hair when I closed my eyes. "Why are you being shown visions about the Watsons? Why them, when they're human and can't hurt us, for one, and for two, why can't I see them?"

"You saw why. I'm their family."

"I'm your significant and we share an ability. There's no reason why I shouldn't be able to see the visions with you."

"Let's just go back to the palace and get on our way back to the states. It's obvious that we're supposed to go to the Watson's compound and do something about this."

"If it even belongs to them anymore." He shrugged. "It was in foreclosure and the last I heard, some wine maker had his eye on it."

"We have to try. I get visions for a reason."

He nodded, leaning forward and kissing my forehead, lingering there to fill me with his touch. "I know, baby."

We made a swift walk to the palace, a silent Lynne and Kyle following behind. When we got there, I informed the council of the strange visions and said I needed to handle them. I kept my mind wide open, listening and digging for anything and everything in their minds. I could hear them. Which meant none of the council members had taken the poultice that Marla and the rest of the Watsons had taken with my blood in it to keep me from hearing their thoughts. So, we didn't know if someone on the council was just really good at hiding it or if we were back to square one with them. Maybe they weren't involved at all and were just really bad at being rulers of our people.

Either way, we were going to the Visionary's library to do some research, and then my family was leaving.

To say they were happy about any of it was a flat-out lie. They said wasting any time on the Watsons was just that, a waste, and my time was better spent elsewhere. When I informed them of the experiments they were performing on humans to give them powers, in turn to try to give themselves powers again, they said humans weren't our concern.

For someone who used to be a human and was tortured by that same family, I was insulted greatly by their lack of compassion. I mean, they had not even an ounce of it. But to not give any concern to the fact that the Watson family was playing a game of trying to get their powers back and the council didn't care? Something had to give.

Caleb followed with silent, stoic steps as we ascended the Visionary's steps to her library. Ashlyn was kept the princess in the tower and the captive, all in one, in this library. I wrapped my arms around myself as I let my eyes search her scrawling on the walls. When I looked back at Caleb, he was watching me carefully. "You okay, baby?"

I nodded. "This could have been me…so easily."

He gulped painfully. "I would have never let them do this to you."

"I know that. But there was no one there to save her. And now, there's no one there to save those people from the Watsons. No one but us. That has to be a reason I got the vision. Maybe…maybe they're going to expose us to a ton of humans or something." I ran my finger along the words on the bricks. "I don't know the whys; I just know that we have to do this."

He engulfed me from behind, his arms around me, his face next to mine on my shoulder. "I'm always with you, whatever you choose to do." He leaned in. "You're the boss, remember?" he said into my ear.

I started to relax, lean into him, when he stiffened.

"What in holy hell is that?" he whispered and let me go gently to move forward, his eyes glued to something on the wall. I saw in his mind the word "Ava" was what he was fixated on. But how was that possible?

"Caleb?" I asked, my voice quivered in the air between us.

He looked back at me and held out his hand. “Come here.” I took it and he pulled me in front of him. “Baby…look.”

There, in the midst of all that gibberish was an infinity symbol made of names. Maggie, Caleb, Kyle, Lynne, Bish, Jen, Haddock, Heather. And then in the middle of all those names was Ava's, her name practically touching another name I’d never heard and didn’t know anyone by that name—Seth.

Who’s Seth?

Four

I looked up at Caleb over my shoulder. *I don't know. But why are our names on this wall, Caleb? Ashlyn didn't know us. Why is our daughter's name in the middle of these names like that?*

He pulled my wrist up, running his thumb over my infinity mark on my tattoo. "I knew it had to mean something."

"Maggie," we heard behind us and we both turned to find Ashlyn. I gasped, unable to stop it. "Maggie," she said again and shook her head in a way that showed her distress. "Oh, Maggie. I'm trying to warn you, but you're not listening."

"I'm listening," I promised her. Now that I knew Ava had something to do with this, there wasn't a Virtuoso member or rule or law that was going to stand in my way of getting to that Watson compound if that was what I was supposed to do. "Please, Ashlyn."

I went and stood right in front of her ethereal form. She still scratched and rubbed at her arms, just like she had in the visions I used to have of her, back when I first came to stay here as the

Visionary before Caleb and I were even married. She looked up at me and then at the wall. She walked to it and pressed her ridged fingers to the middle where Ava's name was and said, "Danger. Danger, Visionary."

Caleb was freaking out, but afraid to speak—afraid to scare her away, so he let me do all the talking.

"What danger? With my daughter? With Ava?"

"You can't see it," she murmured and shook her head harder. She took her nails and slammed them to the wall, digging them deep, and scraped them across the names, Ava's name was almost completely gone. Caleb pulled me back as I gasped. Ashlyn swung around to look at us once more. "Visionary, you know what you saw, you know what has to be done. There's danger. Go, now!"

She disappeared into a wisp of smoke, but the scratch over our daughter's name remained.

"Oh, God. Ava, no," Caleb growled behind me as he took my hand and tugged me to follow him.

We ran. We didn't stop again until we were standing in the doorway of Gran's room, looking at our son and daughter as they played Scrabble with her on the floor. Caleb scooped Ava up and kissed her forehead, murmuring that it was all right. But Ava hadn't known anything was wrong in the first place.

"Daddy, you're squeezing me," she complained.

"I'm sorry, baby girl." He sighed and looked at me over her shoulder, taking my hand and pulling me to him. "Come on, guys. Get your things together. Gran, you, too. Let's get everyone packed up. We're going home."

"I thought-"

"Gran," he begged in a whisper and she knew right then that something was really wrong. "Please."

"All right. Come on, Rodney."

"No, please," I said and picked him up. I hugged him to me and tried my best not to cry. "I just need him with me, okay?"

Her mouth fell open. "Oh, my... Lord, what happened today? Somebody better start talking."

"We will, Gran," Caleb told her and put his arm around my shoulder, kissing my temple, "but first, I want to get on that plane and get my family away from here. We have important things to do."

Two hours later, everyone was on a plane and headed home. As soon as we got to Peter's house, we sat everyone down, the whole Jacobson clan, for an emergency meeting. Caleb took the cog wheel from his pocket, placed it on the table to let them know this was official. He told them everything that was going on—the visions, Ashlyn, what we'd seen and heard and suspected about Ava being in danger and somehow, someway, that it was connected to something the Watsons were doing. They were still conducting experiments on humans and we were told, in no exact words, to do something about that. And that the council wasn't doing anything about any of it.

It was customary for the men to do most of the missions and work in the clan, but when it came to war, all bets were off, Caleb had explained to me once. Their family hadn't had the women fight in a battle in a very long time. Everyone was needed—all hands on deck. They were on board and out the door toward the Watson compound before Caleb could even work up a good angry sweat from his rally-the-troops speech. Gran and a few others stayed with the children, but the majority were going, with the intention of battle.

I changed into some jeans and boots upstairs before we left. Caleb came in and leaned in the doorframe. I couldn't read his mind. He was blocking me, so I assumed he was about to ask me to stay home or stay in the car even. I opened my mouth to argue, but he crossed his arms and sighed before saying firmly, "Stay with me, right by my side. You got me?"

I smiled. "You're not forbidding me to go?"

"Would it work?"

"No," I answered sadly.

He pushed away from the doorframe and came to me, kneeling down and putting my foot on his thigh to finish tying my boot. "Remember the vision you had of us fighting side by side together?" I nodded. He gulped and pulled my laces tight before kneeling up and pushing my knees apart. "So, no, I won't forbid you to go. But please, Maggie, let me protect you. Stay with me, stay connected to me, and listen to me. If I ask you to run or move, don't think. Just do it. I'm keeping you safe, not ordering you around."

I pushed my fingers through his hair, one hand and then the other, as I rubbed his head and tugged gently on his hair. He closed his eyes and leaned in, letting his arms circle my waist as he pressed his cheek to my chest.

"I know you need to keep me safe," I told him, my lips in his hair. "I want you to. We're a team. I can't do this at all if you can't be right there with me. You're the key, remember?"

He sighed and lifted his head. His hands gripped my legs and he tugged me to the edge of the bed to be flush against him. His blue eyes were so heavy and weighed down with everything that was on his mind. I rubbed my thumb over where his dimple should be. It seemed like forever since I'd seen it and it may be an eternity before I would see it again, if this kept up.

"Hey." He lifted my chin, a ghost of a smile there on his sad lips that he was pushing so hard, just for my benefit. "I have a lot to be happy about. They aren't taking anything away from me today. Do you hear me?" I smiled. "Mrs. Jacobson?" he prompted.

I fingered his dimple again. "Yes, Champion. I hear you."

He took my mouth in a painful plea to stay safe above all else. It was hungry and aching and rough, while still being my sweet Caleb that worried. He cupped my neck and dragged me against him, his lips taking mine one at a time, even as he moved his hands to press and caress my back under my shirt to soothe me, fill me with his calm and touch as much as he could before we had to do this and be on our own for this fight.

Then he stood with me in his arms and took one long last pull from my mouth before pulling back. "I could stay here all day, but—"

"Ava," I answered. "I know."

"I am so in love with you," he groaned against my lips, his forehead to mine. "Everything is going to be okay. You're here for a reason. This is happening for a reason. Don't be scared. I believe in you."

"I believe when you believe." I gripped his neck hard with my arms. "I love you, too."

He kissed me once more before setting my feet to the floor. "Let's see the kiddos before we leave."

I nodded and felt my eyes sting. "Don't say anything to make me cry. I don't want to upset her."

He brushed my cheek with his thumb with a sad smile. "Okay."

When we got downstairs, everyone was waiting. The rest of the family had gone to get ready and then brought their children back here so they were all together safely. I knelt in front of Ava and she looked up at me. “You’re leaving now, aren’t you?”

“Yes, baby. We’re going to help some people with some bad men.” I had a thought. “Ava, have you…have you had any weird dreams or anything lately?”

“No, mommy. Not unless us putting Rodney in an all-girls boarding school across the sea for always stealing my dolls and making them his GI Joe prisoners counts.”

Caleb snorted while Gran’s cackle held nothing back. I smiled at her. “Well, I think that’s probably valid.” I hugged her to my chest tightly and tried with everything in me not to cry. “Listen to Gran, okay? And be nice to Rodney. Y’all just play and wait for us to come home. We’ll be back before you know it.”

“Why are you crying? What’s wrong?”

I squeezed my eyes tight. My perceptive girl. I felt Caleb’s hand on my shoulder as he bent down next to me.

“Hey, give Daddy a hug.” He took her from me and I swiped my eyes discreetly. “Mommy just hates it when people hurt other people. We know that, right?” She nodded. “So Mommy and I are going to help somebody. You stay here and help Gran, okay?”

"Okay." She looked down. "Will you be back before bedtime?"

"I hope so."

"Will you sing to me now? In case you don't make it back in time for bedtime?" Her big blue eyes that matched her daddy's looked up at him and I knew he'd sing a hundred songs if that's what she wanted.

He tucked her under his chin and rocked her a little, out of habit, as he leaned back with her and sang "I'm Yours" by Jason Mraz. They did the *doo-doo-doo-doo's* together like they always did. I ached so much in my chest as I watched them. I turned away so she wouldn't see me getting worked up. It wasn't that I didn't have faith in Caleb or myself or what we were or our people…it was just that she was our daughter.

Gran's arms came around me from behind. I didn't have to look to know it was her. I could smell her perfume. "It's going to be all right, pretty girl."

"Is it?" I glanced back at my little girl who Ashlyn told me was in danger somehow. "What if we're playing right into their hands? What if by leaving her today, I'm abandoning her like my mother did me and she'll be stuck without me forever?"

"You know that's not what you saw."

"I've changed my visions before," I countered.

"For the good. For the better. You have your gift for a reason. Ashlyn wouldn't have come to you and told you just to send you to an ambush."

I nodded and breathed deeply through my nose. "You're right."

I turned and hugged her around her neck. The vision hit me when her cool skin touched mine. She gripped me tightly as we watched. Our Gran was older than she was now. She looked so happy—surrounded by her family, tears on her cheeks, her gray hair surrounding her head on the pillow in the upstairs bedroom. She touched Peter's cheek, who tried to keep it together as he looked down at her.

"Oh, Peter," she said and smiled. "Do you have any idea how happy a woman can be in a hundred years?"

He smiled through his tears. "No, Mama. Tell me."

"So happy she'll burst."

He succumbed to his tears and hugged her gently as we all let our Gran go. She smiled all the way to the end. When her hand slowly fell from Peter's head, we knew she was gone. I'd never felt such a peaceful vision before. It was all light and air around me. Gran's goodness touched everything. She truly was the happiest creature that ever touched this earth and she shared it with us every day.

The vision left me and a sob choked in my throat. Gran gripped my cheeks, a smile on her face. "Don't say anything. To anyone."

"Gran—"

"That's the way I would have always wanted to go. Peaceful, surrounded by the people I love. At least I know I won't die by some Watson's hand or in some stupid car. I'll die the right way, the way God intended. Let me have this," she said harder. "This is our secret, pretty girl."

I nodded. What else could I do? She wiped under my eye with her knuckle. "Thank you. You know this family. They won't let it go."

I *did* know. They would drive themselves crazy with worry about it, though it was inevitable that everyone died of old age one day. I nodded again. "I promise."

Five

I tucked Gran's vision away behind my walls and vowed to keep it there. I let my mind return to the matters of the day, to my Ava, which was pretty easy to do, and when Gran and I turned back to the room, they were getting ready to go.

"Mom," Caleb called out, so busy and completely oblivious to my and Gran's revelation. He shook his head. Hearing what he had in his mind, I sighed in relief. "I want you to stay." Rachel's mouth popped open in protest, but Caleb went on. "You're one of the strongest here, your ability could protect the children if someone did come. I want someone to stay here with them, just in case. Don't worry, I'll watch out for Dad."

Rachel was torn. She wanted to keep her grandkids safe, of course, but the significant in her didn't want to send Peter off to fight without her there. Peter was at her side in an instant. He sighed, having heard it all in her mind. "It'll be all right, Rae. Caleb's right. If anyone could stay and protect the children, it would be you."

She took his face in her small hands. "You better be careful."

"Always am." He pulled her up and we looked away as he kissed her.

I kissed Rodney's forehead as he slept in Maria's arms and hugged Ava tight before handing her off to Gran. Gran and I shared a look of understanding before I headed out. It was hard to keep it together for two reasons now. We were on our way before I felt like I even had time to get my bearings. I rode in the front, middle seat with Caleb's hand stuck between my thighs the whole way there as he drove. Peter sat on the other side of me and reached over to squeeze my hand over now and then. It felt like the blink of an eye when we were parking near the woods. When we got out, I was a live wire. I was too worked up. I didn't know what was up or down, what was what.

"Maggie?"

"Huh?" I whispered and lifted just my eyes to find Caleb bending down to catch my gaze. "What?"

He leaned in and kissed my lips firmly, the tips of his fingers rubbing behind my ear. He pushed away from the truck and held his hand out. "Now let's go get these bastards."

It was what I needed. Exactly. I put my hand in his and let him lead me the short walk through the woods to the house. The Watson Compound. I had never seen this part of it when I was here. I could see the well on the cliff a little ways in the back. A shiver ran over me at the thought that we might find people down there today.

"No time like the present," Caleb muttered and lifted his hand to let everyone know, from their various scattered positions across the estate, that we were moving in. There was a couple of cars in the driveway, but for the amount of people that supposedly lived there, it didn't look right. We sneaked across the property line until we reached the main entrance. The massive gate was left cracked open…like they left in a rush. We made our way up the driveway to the house. Some of the family started to search the outlying buildings while we took the main house. Caleb and I took either side of the front door and listened. Not hearing anything, he started to grip the handle to turn it.

I got the worst feeling. I didn't know why, but I hissed, "No."

He stopped. I went to his side and he put me right behind him as he borrowed my ability and yanked the door from hinges with a wrench of his wrist in the air. We turned our heads, just in time it seemed, as a blast of noise and smoke came from the other side of the door. Caleb looked at what it was. "They rigged the door with a shotgun." He looked back at me over his shoulder. "How did you know?"

"I don't know." I gulped.

He squeezed my fingers gently. “It’s okay. They rigged the place since they don’t have any powers to protect themselves.”

“And how is that supposed to make me feel better?”

He didn’t answer as he inched past the gun and looked around the room. “If they were here, they would have heard that. We need to move quickly.”

“The well,” I said. “And the bunker out on the hill.”

He nodded. He knew I was right. If they had someone here, that’s where they were keeping them. We moved over the hill to the storm shelter looking door and opened it up to find the ladder leading down to the tunnels as Kyle and Lynne went for the well. I gasped at the smell. It smelled the same…exactly the same.

Caleb held the door open as our family watched and waited for instruction. Peter was next to me and gripped my arm to keep me steady. Caleb walked to me easily. They all knew and remembered what happened to me here. “You don’t have to go down there. You can stay out here and—”

“No,” I cut him off. “Then they win.” I looked up at Peter and back to Caleb’s eyes, begging him to give me the strength to do this. “Sikes doesn’t get to win, does he? Marcus doesn’t get to win after everything they did?”

He touched my cheek. “Hell no.”

"Let's go."

I let him go first because I knew he needed to, but I was anxious now. I needed to see if anyone was down there and get them out of there if they were. While half the family stood topside and watched for company, walking the estate, the rest of us came down and started to search the tunnels. I opened my mind and listened, but it was quiet.

It didn't take long however to know that we'd found what we were looking for. When a ghost white hand crept out from the bars of a cell, so weak the fingers could barely bend, I yelled for the person to back away so I could open the door. With the only weapon I had, I used my mind to yank the door from the hinges to reveal a woman so thin and weak, I didn't know how she was still alive.

She was afraid, I could tell, but Caleb immediately knelt and lifted her, handing her to someone closer to the hall and told her it was okay, that we were taking her somewhere safe. Her cries and "Thank you"s could be heard all the way down the tunnel. Every door we opened, another woman, another man was found. Some were hardly abused at all and you could tell they were taken care of and then others were barely alive. It made no sense at all. We rescued over fourteen people from those rooms. They said the Watsons had just been there that morning, so we missed them by a couple hours.

When we went inside the house and searched the rooms, we didn't find anyone inside, but we did find more booby-traps. We decided we'd wait them out, but when we started finding cameras in every room, we knew there was more to it. I sighed, knowing we'd missed them, knowing they weren't coming back. They were probably watching us right that minute. I took one of the cameras Caleb had ripped down in my hand and didn't flinch when the vision came.

They scattered. They had gotten smart. In the absence of powers, they didn't roll over and play human like we thought—no. They had taken the initiative to use power that was manmade while they worked on Sikes' formula. So they studied technology and tactical systems to keep themselves safe until the time came when they could get their true powers back. They had gotten good at pretending, blending in, being invisible. We had practically forgotten they existed.

And that was our mistake.

We should have checked up on them and made sure that they were giving up. Now, they knew we knew their secret, so they scattered all over so we couldn't find them.

But they weren't finished.

One day, they'd be back to finish what they started. They still had every intention of creating a serum that would make them Virtuoso again, either by imprinting or other means.

We were too late. But at least we saved those people.

I yanked out of the vision and shook my head, disappointed and happy at the same time. “They’re gone,” I told everyone. “They planted the cameras to see if someone found them and knew we were here. They aren’t coming back.”

They started to cheer, but when they saw that I wasn’t as happy and Caleb came to soothe me, running his fingers over my Visionary mark on my neck, they slowed their celebration.

“Why don’t you seem happy about that?” Kyle asked.

“If they were here now, we could end it now,” Caleb explained, knowing I was exhausted in my head. “Now, we’ll have to wait, look over our shoulder, wait for them to snatch more humans and use them for guinea pigs to finish the experiment. They won’t stop until they get what they want.”

Everybody seemed to understand then.

“Let’s do one last search before we leave, make sure we didn’t miss anything,” Caleb ordered.

I crossed my arms and looked around the room we were in one last time. There was nothing remarkable there. It was a typical American house. The couch matched the curtains, the floors were wood, and the chandelier in the foyer bounced the light from the setting sun out of the window onto the walls. It was a beautiful place. It was a shame that people, so evil, had lived there.

Some kid's artwork caught my eye on the way out. It was over the fireplace. I smiled, thinking of my own kids, knowing that they would be safe now, for a while anyway. It seemed strange that people so evil would be thoughtful and caring enough to want to show off their son's artwork like this.

He had drawn a boy on a horse for one, then the other was a woman holding hands with a little boy on the hillside. I felt hands on my shoulders and looked up at Caleb.

"Hey…what?" His face was white as a sheet.

"Maggie, look at these drawings."

"I see them. What?"

He pointed to the name on top. I don't know how I missed it. "Seth."

"Oh, my… What does this mean?" I turned and looked at him frantically. "Ashlyn warned us. Did we miss something?"

"Come on." He snatched the drawings from the mantel, and we hurried to the truck where a few of the rescued people were still sitting, waiting for us to leave. "Was there a child down in the cells with you?" he asked them.

"No," the fragile woman answered. I sighed, but before I could relax, she broke my heart in two. "He doesn't stay down there with us, they keep him in the house. My cell neighbor had him several years ago, but they…got rid of her. They raise him now. They bring him down to the cells sometimes. They tell him we're criminals."

"Caleb," I said, knowing we failed. "She said I wasn't seeing it properly. She told me!"

He took me and hugged me hard to his chest, sighing into my hair. "Baby, it's not your fault they ran with him. Look at all these people you saved."

"He's just a little boy." I sniffed.

"We'll keep looking," he promised and kissed my forehead. "We won't stop looking for him."

When we got back home, we took the rescues to the hospital. Some of the family members thought it might be exposing our kind if they talked, but honestly, they would just think it was a crazy family that kidnapped them. Fact was, the Watsons had no powers. The police crawled all over that place, but found nothing to lead them to where the Watsons were. They eventually just left it, abandoned, a crime scene with no leads. Somehow, the Watsons had gotten the money to pay the mortgages they were behind on, barely, so they owned the land again outright.

We just had to wait for them to return to it.

All the children were asleep when we finally got home that night. Caleb and I just crawled into the big bed in Caleb's old room with them and held on tight. I couldn't help but cry for

Seth, a little boy I didn't even know. I had failed him. Even though Caleb tried to soothe me and take all my hurt away, I knew it was all my fault.

The next morning, I snuck out of the arms and limbs in my bed and Gran, Rachel, and I made pancakes for everyone. It was a full house at Peter's, but even still, I didn't have the energy to change out of my pineapple pajama shorts and t-shirt the kids bought me for my birthday last year. I heard Caleb's thoughts when he woke up, so I started making his coffee with mine. I fingered the hem of my shorts while the coffee brewed. I wondered if Seth even knew who his mother was.

Hands gripped my waist. "You've got to stop doing this to yourself, baby," he drawled into the back of my neck before kissing the skin there. "You can't blame yourself for the actions of others."

I turned and faced him, sighing at the sight of him. I bit my lip and ran my hand through his hair to help him tame it. "Morning," I whispered.

"Are you trying to rile me up this morning?" he asked, his voice that low, husky tone usually reserved for a flight of stairs above us. He ran his fingers along the seam of my short's leg. "Pancakes, coffee, and…pineapple shorts?"

I gave him the small smile he was looking for. He gave me the dimples I wanted in return. I closed the small distance between us and right as our lips touched, our new wonderful life interrupted us.

"Ew, Daddy."

We both looked over at Rodney who was half smiling, half barf-faced.

"Ew?" Caleb asked. "Ew, really?" He laughed as he scooped him up and threw him over his shoulder. He came back to me. "We'll finish this later, Mommy."

I smiled and giggled. "Yes, Daddy."

He kissed me loudly, smacking my butt as he walked away.

"Ew, ew, ew!" Rodney chanted as Caleb trotted away with him laughing.

We ate breakfast all together, spirits lifted. Everyone felt this victory in their very souls, so I tried with everything in me to portray my happiness with them since they all looked to me to lead them. And I *was* happy, I just knew it wasn't over. And the fact that it was a helpless child I had failed was making the guilt multiply.

Later that night, we went back to our home. After dinner, we watched a movie with Ava and Rodney, anything to keep them with us and not leave them alone.

Ava blurted out of nowhere. "Did you see Seth yesterday, Daddy?"

I froze. Caleb turned to her slowly and gave her a little smile, trying his best to look normal. "Who? Who's Seth, Ava?"

"Ashlyn told me about him. She told me you'd save him. She said that he would be my friend one day." She looked up from her cookies and milk with the most innocent, hopeful look. "Did you save him, Daddy?"

Caleb was stunned silent. Ava went on. "I know you saw him, Daddy." She hopped down and went into his coat pocket, grabbing the drawings that we'd taken from the Watson's. "See?" She laid it on the table and pointed to the boy and the woman on the hill. "This is Seth and this is Ashlyn."

"How do you know this, baby girl?" he asked as he hoisted her up in his arms.

This was in my pocket all night, Maggie.

"Ashlyn told me," Ava answered, like she was getting exasperated. "She said you were going to save him."

"Sweetheart, I…" My heart literally broke right there. Why was Ashlyn doing this? Why was she messing with our children when it was just going to break their hearts if something went wrong? I didn't understand. "I'm so sorry, Ava."

I moved close to hug her, but the second I touched her skin, I was blinded by white light. I heard Caleb's gasp, so I knew he was with me on this one. Ava giggled. "It's just Ashlyn. She won't hurt you."

And then Ashlyn was there. She didn't look real here. She looked like a dream or a ghost. She smiled. It was genuine and it was the first time I'd seen her where she didn't look like she was going insane. "Ashlyn?"

"I'm sorry, Maggie. I know you're probably upset. But this is the only way I get any peace." She smiled at Ava. "And Ava is so sweet and so fun to be with. And Rodney. And…Seth."

I sighed. Caleb's arm around me tightened. "Ashlyn, just tell us what's going on."

"I can't leave the palace. I'm stuck there. When your children were born, that was the first time since I died that I was able to leave, to get any peace from the madness that I've felt ever since Richard and I were supposed to imprint and weren't allowed to. I don't know why, I don't know how, but I can come visit them and they're the only ones that can see me." She nodded and smiled. "Unless you touch them and have a vision at the same time."

"So…" my heart lifted, "you can still talk to Seth?"

She pursed her lips. "It takes a lot of energy to come, so I can only come once every few days. And I've noticed that the older the children have gotten over the years, the less often they see me. Sometimes I come and they don't notice me. Which makes me think that soon, they won't notice at all."

“Why?” Caleb said when I couldn’t. “What purpose other than you wanting to get out of the palace?”

“I promise you I never wanted to hurt anyone. I just wanted to spend time with them. And you. Even though you couldn’t see me, your family gave me some semblance of what my family use to be like.” The wistful look on her face was heartbreaking. “But then I saw those people that the Watsons were keeping and had to get you to save them. It was the only way to save Seth.”

“But I didn’t save him, Ashlyn.” A sob caught in my throat. “We were too late. Seth’s gone. I didn’t save him.” I looked down at Ava. “I’m sorry, baby.”

“Visionary,” Ashlyn called loudly and squinted at me, “your job is done. Everything you should have accomplished was done so.”

I shook my head at her, my mouth open. “No. They have Seth. I didn’t get to him in time.”

“I never said to take him away from them, I said to save him.” I scoffed, angry at her statement. What games was she playing with me? She came forward and smiled genuinely. “Even now you doubt yourself.” I pressed my lips together. “Don’t,” she said harder. “You are who you are for a reason. I sent you there to save all those people from the Watsons. That in turn will save Seth.”

"I don't understand."

"They were grooming him to be a monster like them. Now, their course is altered, their choices, different. They must do something different in their journey to find what they're looking for, and I see a different path for our Seth. One that will lead him back to us."

"What do you see?"

"I can't tell you. But I'll tell you this—we'll see him again." She smiled and tapped the end of Ava's nose with her finger. "You'll see."

"Promise?" Ava begged. "You said he would be my friend one day?"

"He will, Ava. Promise."

"So what about me?" I asked. "I'm supposed to just forget about that little boy and let them raise him, not look for him, not try to find him and take him?"

"When he's ready, he'll find you."

"Then what?"

"Then, you can save him. He'll need you." She looked at Ava. "He'll need you, too." She stood straighter. "In the meantime, you know what you have to do."

Before she even finished the sentence, I knew what she meant. The council. The council was history. She nodded and smiled. "And you know who will replace them." My mouth opened in surprise that I hadn't seen it before. *There, in the midst of all that gibberish was an infinity symbol made of names. Maggie, Caleb, Kyle, Lynne, Bish, Jen, Haddock, Heather.* She nodded again. "Yes. All is as it should be, Visionary. You are right where you should be. It's just a matter of getting it done."

I sighed, not wanting the task of firing council members at all, ever, in the least. "And then what, Ashlyn?"

"And then…war, Visionary. War."

The End

...for now

Be sure to continue on to the next book in this series, Undeniably Chosen. A sneak has been provided for you in the back of this book.

Turn the page for a sneak of the next book in the Significance series

Undeniably Chosen

One

Ava

I waited for that day, for that one thing to complete me. To feel someone's heartbeat inside my chest and know that it was reciprocated. To find the one who belonged to me and could be the one to make me whole.

I still waited. I was a sophomore in high school. Graduating and heading off to U of T in a just two years so I could be an architect, just like Grandpa.

We just got back from the last reunification. Mom had taken fire for her new rule about the Visionary being able to work and have a day job rather than just...being the Visionary. They wanted her to be 'accessible' at all times and she warred on that she could be accessible and still work with Daddy at the centers as well. That's what cell phones were for.

So I watched as Dad was being extra nice and attentive by cooking dinner that night since, even though she was the Visionary, it sucked when people were against you and questioned your dedication.

Wanna know what else sucked? Being the Visionary's daughter. And the clan leader's daughter deducted even more points.

I loved my parents, don't get me wrong. They were great. Rodney and I both were pretty grounded. We went to the private school here and he played football while I played volleyball. I'd been working at the learning centers for Daddy for a year now.

I loved it, but planned to go work for Grandpa as soon as I graduated from college. Dad was fine with it. He of all people knew what it was like to want to be something, to have the fire for something.

I was fascinated by the thought that I could create something like that.

We used to travel around with Daddy's job, staying in a place for a couple months before moving on to the next place. It might not sound so appealing, but it really was amazing to live in all those states. We lived in New York, Washington, Chicago, Texas, and about fifteen other states. But, when I was almost in high school, they wanted us to settle down, so we moved back to Tennessee and Daddy bought Mom a big, beautiful red house with a wraparound white porch. Rodney's old fort made from wood slats was still in the backyard, though he hadn't been back there in years.

It was our home and I loved it, but also couldn't wait to leave it. My teenage heart was so fickle. But the one thing it wasn't fickle on was wanting my significant.

So, back to the part where I was waiting. Even though I wasn't of age yet, every reunification brought anxiousness for me. I was fifteen. Mom was only seventeen when she imprinted and since all the rules were being broken, I couldn't help but hope that I would imprint soon.

It was more than just wanting to have somebody, it was like this thing in my body was pulled just a little too tight. Just enough to annoy and bother me, but not enough to be painful. My significant was the only one who could make me feel normal. I knew it.

Dad tossed the noodles with the white sauce, Mom's favorite, and divided it onto four plates as our new puppy Mavis rubbed against my leg. Dad glanced up at me with a smile. "Put ice in some glasses for me, sweetheart?"

"Sure."

"Rodney. Rodney!" he called louder.

Rodney took his earphones out and looked at him. "Yeah?"

"Silverware."

"Why are you cooking again?" he asked. "Mom's a way better cook than you."

"Hey!" Dad laughed and slung a noodle at him. It landed on Rodney's face and hair.

He jumped back like that would save him, but it was too late. "Dude!" he shrieked, his voice cracking with puberty as he swatted at his shagged hair. "Dude, my hair!"

Dad and I were laughing so hard, we could barely stand up as Rodney went on. Rodney jumped across the counter and stuck his finger in the sauce before holding it out to Dad. "You're gonna get it, old man."

I ducked out of the way, fearful of my own hair, and giggled by the fridge as they fought and wrestled. I felt Mom's hands on my arms and heard her laugh behind me. "Oh, my. Ava, what's going on?"

"Dad pulled the unforgiveable. He got noodles in Rod's hair."

She giggled and came around me with her blue silk robe on and bare feet. "Is all this for me?" she crooned sweetly, looking around at the mess on the counter.

"Mom, totally his fault." Rodney pointed at Dad shamelessly as he laughed.

"Oh, I believe you." She wrapped her arms around Dad's neck and wiped a smidge of sauce from his cheek with her thumb.

"You believe him over me?" Daddy asked, his voice changing like it always did where Mom was concerned.

She laughed, reaching up on her tiptoes and kissed him. "Thank you for cooking dinner. You didn't have to."

"I wanted to," he replied. His voice and eyes held a reverence that I'd always seen and heard about my whole life, but never experienced. "You earned it. You're such a good woman, and I know the reunifications take it out of you."

I had watched my parents for what seemed like centuries. The way they existed so effortlessly in each other's world and space. They could go minutes without looking away from each other. They kissed constantly. They hugged all the time, stole touches and wrapped their fingers around the other's wrist. I knew it was to feel their calm, to be wrapped in the little bit of bliss that their touch provided.

I felt like I was watching a romance novel play out before my eyes.

"I'm OK," she told him and whispered her next words. "Thank you for this. And for earlier. I really needed it."

"Eew. Gross. Stop," Rodney said, hands up. He threw some forks haphazardly on the table. "Don't you see the way my ears are singed?"

Mom laughed. "I was talking about the bubble bath your father made me, you goober." She reached up again, kissing Daddy on the lips, but he reached around her and drew her in even more. I turned to fill the glasses. It was disgusting, they were my parents after all, but I was also envious. Things were still a little up in the air with the imprints and everything. It seemed that things had gone back to normal for the most part, except there were no more age limits. You met them when you met them and that was that.

So instead of knowing I'd meet the person I wanted most in a few years while in college, I was forced to spend my days *waiting.*

The only thing a girl in high school, who's never dated anyone before, wants is to find someone to love her. I was breaking out and going my own way, and while I was reinventing myself to become the me I would always be, I was dying to throw my epic love story in the mix.

"I love you, Maggie," I heard behind me.

"I love you more."

"Go sit. I'll bring you a plate." And I waited for it...

The sound of Daddy's palm lightly smacking Mom's butt was my cue that it was okay to turn around now. Mom shook her head at Dad as she took a seat. Dad, smug as all get out, brought her plate, kissing her forehead as he sat it in front of her, before setting the rest of the table and playfully yelling at Rodney to sit down and behave like a Jacobson.

They were so predictable. And adorable. And so in love with each other it hurt to look at them.

Two

Six Years Later
Ava

I yawned and got the stink eye from Professor Gracco. I loved and hated class, but it was the last week of them before summer break. Every class was a yawn-fest. The teachers knew it, but I think it just made them that much more ornery.

The minutes crawled by and my watch kept winking at me, taunting, begging me to keep looking at it so the time would move even slower.

Only two more years of this and I'd graduate and could go work at the firm with Grandpa. Well, not for very long because he was retiring in a few years. But the chance to work with him at all would be worth it. He was happy that I'd decided to come work with them. A few other family members had taken a cue from Dad and went their own way, running a business that they wanted instead.

But they always seemed to be good businesses. Our kind had a knack for smart ventures and risks that paid off. Businesses that were good for more than just us. Like Daddy with his learning centers and my second cousin, who has a horse farm, who started an equestrian riding school.

When the professor took the little golden bell from his desk and jiggled it in the air at us like it was a catholic school and not a college, we knew the class was over. I packed up my things hurriedly and rushed across campus to the coffee shop. Every Friday I brought the whole staff at the center whatever poison that was their favorite beverage.

I was running late. Professor Hubris back there thought that he held our literal futures in his sweaty little hands and it was his duty to teach more than what was lined out in the syllabus.

Like maybe, how to make someone late for work? It didn't matter that my dad owned the company. That actually made me want to be on time even more, so no one could say that I was just there because my father let me be. I wanted to be a good worker, have ethics and values that people could see on me like a Girl Scout badge.

I wanted to earn what I had, not have things handed to me.

So when I ran into the shop and saw Paul at the counter with a carton of coffee cups, I mouthed a 'Thank you' to him. I got the same exact thing every Friday. One white hot chocolate, one black, one vanilla cappuccino with cream and sugar, and for me, a salted caramel iced coffee. There was a long line today, so I waited in it, pulling out my cell to check messages quickly.

A napkin floated to the floor beside me and I reached absentmindedly to pick it up when someone was next to me doing the same thing. Our fingers almost touched on the napkin and my eyes lifted to see dark ones meeting mine. I felt my lips part, not just at his closeness, but at the sheer force of that gaze.

His hair was black and spiked up in the middle in a small faux-hawk. He was tan with a red t-shirt that hugged his neck.

"Thanks," he muttered, his voice as low as gravel. I had to admit that it made me smile for no other reason than the fact that he hadn't taken his eyes off mine yet. He finally, slowly stood.

"No problem," I replied and cleared my throat a little because my voice sounded entirely too affected.

I didn't know what else to say and he just stared, his eyes wandering around my face, before he finally smiled with just one side of his mouth and chuckled a little. "Sorry...you're just really..." He shook his head and stepped back. "Never mind. You go to school here?"

"Yeah. You?"

"Nah," he said, noncommittally. "Just getting some coffee. It was pretty good timing, I guess."

"What was?" I asked, shouldering my bag, refusing to let him go until it was no longer polite to keep him talking.

"Coming here at the same time as you." His smile spoke volumes of things he was thinking that I wasn't privy to. It reminded me of a romance novel...of my parents. I felt a stutter in my chest at what that could mean. "I'm usually here a lot later, but I was early today."

"You're early and I'm late," I said, chagrined that I had forgotten my purpose so easily. I looked over to the counter to see Paul staring an irritated yet intrigued look at my back. I knew he had a little crush on me, but there was no point in pursuing that.

I turned back to dark eyes. He whispered like it was a curse, "Am I keeping you? Do you need to go?"

I stepped off the plank, one hopeful foot in front of the other. "Do you feel that?"

He frowned with his brows, but smiled. "Feel what exactly?"

My spirits fell as fast as they had risen. This was just some college boy checking out girls in the coffee shop. He wasn't Virtuoso, he wasn't a human so intrigued by what was happening to him to press further, and he wasn't someone...that I could go any further with.

I smiled as much as I could, but stepped back. "I really do have to go. I’m sorry. I'm really late."

His smile fell and he took a step closer. "Uh...can you stay for one cup of coffee? I'm buying." He tried for a smile again, but I just couldn't let this go any farther.

"I'm late for work already." I turned to give Paul a twenty and told him to keep the change. When I turned back, I expected dark eyes to be gone, done with me, but he wasn't. I smiled and started to move around him toward the side back door.

He called for me to wait a second as he ran back to get his bag from the table, but I kept going. Before I reached the door, his hand gently caught my long sleeve in his fingers. I looked down at his hand first and then at his face. "I'm sorry," he said sincerely. "I'm not trying to be creepy, I just..." He licked his lips.

His red shirt had a fireman symbol on the front with the number 22 in the middle of it. His jeans were dark, worn, and ripped a little at the knee. He wore black boots and had a brown leather band around his wrist that had the word VIVERE on it.

Wow, this boy was going to be a problem if I didn't get away.

"I know. I wish I had time to talk, I really do, but I have to go."

"I do feel it," he said in a harsh voice. "I said I didn't feel it before, but I do."

Every movement but breathing stopped. "Feel what?"

"Like..." He moved his hand to my face and I froze in hopeful awe. He swept my hair back behind my ear. "Like we were meant to be here at the same time."

It was when his finger touched the rim of my ear that I felt my life changing before my eyes. He sucked in a huge breath right along with me and immediately I felt his hands on both sides of my face, pulling me in to press his forehead to mine as we watched the scenes play out. I worried about him. He must be a human because I'd never seen him before and was probably freaking out, but all I could do in that second was cling to his shirt with my empty hand, fisting the fabric and hanging on as I watched our future life together.

In one vision, we were lying in the tall grass somewhere. He ran his fingers up and down my arm. I talked and he listened like his life depended on it. The next one was us as we walked hand in hand down the sand at the beach house my parents owned. He had a bandage across his neck and his arm was in a sling, but he smiled so wide as he looked down at me, black eye and all. And then the third came, us in front of a big house. It was a place that looked familiar, but we stood there, older in our years, proud...like we belonged there on the big lawn and grand landscapes that seemed overgrown, but once beautiful. He was kissing my lips so softly.

We eased out of our reverie and his smile wasn't one of a human, it was one of someone who knew exactly what was going on. He moved us gently, pressing my back to the wall by the back door, but kept my face blissfully captive in his warm hands that I just knew were big and hard-worked calloused. "Oh, my g... It can't be," he said, but his smile refuted those words. "It's...really you."

"And I don't even know your name," I whispered in return.

He chuckled a little, deep and heady. "Seth."

"I'm Ava," I answered before he could ask.

"Ava," he repeated and I felt shivers run over me. He smiled, moving a little closer before letting his forehead touch mine once more. "I can't believe this is happening."

"I don't have to wait anymore," I realized. Even with school and work and everything going on, I was constantly waiting for this. It consumed a little piece in the back of my brain and I was subconsciously always looking for the one whose touch would bind me to him and also set me free.

His smile faltered a little as he leaned his head back. "So...you're Virtuoso."

I nodded. "How come I've never seen you before?"

"We don't...go to the reunifications," he muttered softly. He looked so nervous and I felt the need to comfort him wash over me.

I still held the carton of coffee in one hand so I un-fisted his shirt and reached for his face. I was utterly shocked at how easily it came to me to be with him already. "Hey. What's the matter?"

"I just..." He shook his head and gulped, covering my hand with his on his cheek, like he wanted to keep it there forever. "I don't want to hurt you. I don't want... Gah, I'm so sorry, Ava."

"For what?" I said, but I saw in his mind for the first time. He was thinking about that house from my last vision. I realized that I remembered it from our histories. Our family taught about that...house...

The coffee cups fell from my hand. It was then the world came back to me and I saw several of the people in the coffee shop staring at us. Even Paul had stopped making coffee and was looking at us, like maybe he wanted to intervene.

I pushed Seth's chest a tiny bit, my hands aching and scolding me for doing so. He went without a fight. "Ava," he reasoned, pleaded.

"I've got to go." I turned to go, my heart banging in my chest.

He grabbed my hand gently, his calm, the very thing I'd always wanted, shot through me and I couldn't stop the sigh, yet I still yanked my hand away. "Ava, please. Let's just talk for a minute."

I burst through the door and ran to my Volvo parked in front. Seth followed me, but didn't try to stop me. I got in and shut the door, pressing the push-start button crank the car. He stood outside my window, gripping his hair in his hands as he watched me back out. I heard him in my head as I peeled from the lot.

I'll wait for you however long you need. It's okay. I understand. I'd hate me, too.

I loved his voice. It ran over me like a silk nightgown...and I hated and loved that.

I went straight to the center, blowing through the doors, tears running down my face. Everyone stopped what they were doing and stared, but I looked for Daddy. When I didn't see him with any of the kids, I went right to his office. He was on the phone, but hung up on whoever was on the phone as soon as he saw me.

"Ava—"

"Daddy," I sobbed.

He stood quickly. "What happened?"

"I...imprinted..."

"You did?" he grinned and hugged me to him. "That's amazing, Ava. Where? Who? Why are you crying? Was it—"

"No, Daddy, no." I leaned back.

"What's the matter, baby?" he soothed and smoothed my hair like he had done for my entire life. Always comforting, always willing to bust heads if need be to make me happy. But Dad couldn't fix this.

"Daddy, I imprinted...with a Watson."

Available now!

Playlist

Drive All Night : NeedToBreathe

Who's Gonna Save Us : Gavin DeGraw

Durban Skies : Bastille

I'm Yours : Jason Mraz

Every Night : Imagine Dragons

Make It To Me : Manchester Orchestra

Royals : Lorde

Morning Song : The Lumineers

Shelly is a *New York Times* & *USA Today* bestselling author from a small town in Georgia and loves everything about the south. She is wife to a fantastical husband and stay at home mom to two boisterous and mischievous boys who keep her on her toes. They currently reside in scorching North Florida. She loves to spend time with her family, binge on candy corn, go out to eat at new restaurants, buy paperbacks at little bookstores, sight-see in the new areas they travel to, listen to new music everywhere, and LOVES to read.

Her own books happen by accident and she revels in the writing and imagination process. She doesn't go anywhere without her notepad for fear of an idea creeping up and not being able to write it down immediately, even in the middle of the night, when her best ideas are born.

Shelly's website:

www.shellycrane.blogspot.com

https://www.facebook.com/shellycranefanpage

https://twitter.com/AuthShellyCrane

Shelly's other series or books

Significance series

Oxygen series

Devoured series

Wide Awake series

Collide series

Smash Into You

Shelly also writes a series for inspiration adult romance under the pen name. Shelby Fallon

Stolen Hearts series

Now, enjoy an excerpt from
Shelly Crane's new book, *THE OTHER SIDE OF GRAVITY.*
Betrayal, suspense, and as always, a spine-bending love story.
Available now!

Prologue

"**C**old?" I asked even as I reached across her to check and to see if her built-in warmer was on. It wasn't.

She pushed my arm away. "I've got it."

I held my hands up. "Just wanted to make sure you were warm enough. It's freezing out here."

"I can take care of myself," she muttered and then seemed to gather steam, tightening her arms around herself. "I hope you don't think that just because we kissed that you can just…"

"I can just what?"

She looked over at me for a second before looking back to the path we were walking. It was full of people, but she didn't seem to see a one of them. "You're not my new Lord. You're not my new proprietor, my new master, my new…" She gritted her teeth.

I felt my bones go numb. "Go ahead, Sophelia. Let me have it." I purposely said her full name, knowing she'd notice. She was pulling away, trying to show me the girl she could be. That snarky girl from the ship was making a comeback. But what she didn't know was that strong, independent girl was just as much of a turn on as the soft Sophelia that I've had the past week. But she was forgetting how strong and courageous she was standing up in front of that camera, in front of the Militia when she was running out of air. She was always strong, always courageous, and she was always brave and smart. The loving, caring, amazingly beautifully-hearted girl I'd come to know was just lurking under the surface. And it didn't take that much digging to find her. She wasn't two people. She wasn't a puzzle that needed solving, she was one amazing girl who just didn't know it yet.

"I'm a plague," she whispered.

"Oh, my… Soph."

"I am!" she screamed, surprising me. "I *am* a plague. I have taken down plenty of people so far." She scoffed bitterly. "You don't want to be with me, Maxton." She wouldn't look at me. She just shook her head at the ground. "I'm a destroyer of goods things. Of good people." She finally looked up. "You have family who needs you—"

"That I can't go home to. You know that. I won't bring the things I've done into my family's life. It was my decision to do them, before you even came along, and now I'll pay the price."

"You could still be near them at least."

"Next door or a million miles away." I shrugged. "If you can't talk to or see the ones you love, what does it matter?"

She closed her eyes, searching her brain for new evidence, I assumed. "I got you fired."

"I turned you in for the reward. Twice." I put up two fingers to drive my point home.

She growled. I heard the twins scoffing and making noises at our banter. They had stopped a few feet behind us, knowing better than to come closer.

Her eyes were fierce as hell as she gazed up at me, telling me to run as fast as I could away from her and begging me to stay all in the same blink.

"They will always be after you if you're with me." Her bottom lip started to quiver, her tell that it was all crashing down, but she kept up her fierce face. Her fists were clenched at her sides. "You'll never be safe. You'll never be free to walk the streets without," she fingered the appearance scrambler around her neck, "these things on!" she yelled. "You'll be a prisoner. You'll be *my* prisoner!"

A few people walking by on the street had noticed her outburst and were giving us weird looks as they passed, but nobody seemed to care for more than a fleeting second, more worried about whatever mundane things were going on in their own lives.

"Don't you care?" she yelled. "Don't you care that your life will be over? Don't you care that I'm taking everything from you?" She looked over at the twins. "You, too. Run! Run while you still can. You shouldn't be here." That lip… "You shouldn't want to be with me. I'm a plague that will take everyone down with me. I'm damaged, I'm slashed and scarred, I'm cracked…" That lip lost its fight as finally her lips parted and a small sob made its way through.

I came into her space, done with this whole thing. That lip was my undoing.

"You listen to me, Soph," I growled, but took a breath, taking it down a notch. I lifted her face with a crooked finger under her chin, wanting nothing more than to kiss her trembling mouth and make everything bad in her life go away for good. But life didn't work that way, did it? You couldn't think happy thoughts and fly away to Neverland. And you couldn't kiss girls and have everything in their life that was wrong be right. If only. But I was apparently doing something right, because that lip…it wasn't trembling quite as much anymore. And her eyes? They begged me to save her. "You were slashed when I found you, remember? And now, you have some scars." Her face crumpled and she tried to move it away from my hand, but I brought it back to face me. I wrapped my free hand around her back, right against the part of her I was speaking of, and brought her against me. I put my mouth against her ear. "What is a life without scars? Scars come in all forms and we all have them. Some deeper than others, some more than others, some harsher than others. Your scars are *yours*, Soph, and you *earned* them," I said harshly, my lips touching the rim of her ear. "It felt like sh—awful going through what you did, but the point is you did it. You. No one else. And no one else could have but you. And your scars are beautiful because of who you are and what you did to earn them. Don't ever be ashamed of them. As for you being a plague? If that's so, then please, infect me. Because I want everything you've got to give me." I was pleased to hear a sniffled small laugh.

I leaned back, still holding her chin. There were a few tears clinging to the place under her eyes. I took her face in my hands, ten percent surprised that she let me and ninety percent elated that she was back to the brave, loving girl who took her destiny by the balls and said to hell with her past. I wiped her tears with my thumbs, somehow loving how she closed her eyes when I did so. It made it seem that much more special somehow.

She opened her eyes and I finished my speech.

"And you may be a little cracked, Soph, but it wouldn't take very much to fix them. And I'd love to try."

She smiled, looking at my shirtfront, and sighed. "Why did you have to be so amazing?"

I laughed a little. "Well, I could give you a list—"

She smacked my gut and I "oomphed" for her benefit. She lifted her eyes to mine and I saw the question before she asked. "Why are you doing this? What do you get out of it? I'm…I'm not worth the trouble of all this, of the trouble that is coming for us—for me."

I hoped it showed on my face. I couldn't see how it wasn't. I felt it in that moment as I thought about the way I felt when I was with her, when she had been with my family, when she tugged on my hair in that way she does, when she joked with the twins and laughed so wholeheartedly, when she kissed me back like we wouldn't wake up the next day so she'd better make it good. I smiled and brought her closer a little, my hand still holding her face.

"The fact that you can't see how much you're worth makes you worth so much more." She opened her mouth once, her brow bunched, but nothing came out. She didn't know the words to ask. I continued. "A diamond doesn't know how much it's worth; it's just beautiful because it exists."

Sophelia

"That doesn't go with the common metals, it goes with the silvers. How long have you been working here?" she quipped, her black hair still shiny from wherever she came from. She hadn't been here long enough for this life to taint her mind and body yet. But it would.

"Working here would imply some form of payment, Helga. And payment is something I've never received. Just call it what it is." I turned to look at her again. "You're the new one here. I've been *here* longer than I've been free. So don't tell me what I know and don't know about this place. It goes with the commons because that's what it is." I turned the basket toward her and showed her the goods anyway. "See?" I picked a big chunk up with the magnet hanging on the basket. "All common metals. Now get back to work on your side before Rivers come back."

She grinned evilly. "You said "work". I thought we didn't work here—"

"Just shut up and finish."

She groaned as she walked over to her side. "I'm so hungry I could eat the tail off of a horsopotomus."

"Gross. And stop." My stomach grumbled as she talked about food, even if it was about eating the Militia's riding units.

I rolled my eyes. I couldn't complain really. I had it better than other slaves. At least I wasn't in the mines. They never saw the sun and they never got much food, just enough to keep them going, from what I heard anyway.

At least I got to eat three meals a day. They may not be the meals I wanted to eat, but they were meals. Of sorts. The door slammed upstairs and Helga seized up so violently that her basket spilled.

I rushed over. "Helga," I hissed. "You can't do things like this."

"I'm sorry," she said, rushing to help me throw the pieces of metal back into her basket. We both knew what it meant to not finish our work, let alone spilling or damaging the goods. My fingers were cutting against the sharp edges of the metal shards, but I kept tossing them in as quickly as I could. The basement door opened and then my heart seized as well. There were still pieces on the floor.

She stood and grabbed my basket, rushing to stand a few feet away in front of her work station. I glared up at her, but she refused to meet my eyes; just looked ahead stoically.

"You know what he'll do to me," I whispered as I continued to pick up her pieces.

She kept her eyes forward and whispered back harshly. "Better you than me."

I'd never been so ashamed of my kind before. Helga had been with us for three weeks now and I'd done nothing but help her and show her all the ways to avoid Rivers' wrath, and this was how my kindness was repaid? Traitorism?

"There's a special place for traitors in the underworld," I hissed before standing and putting my feet over the pieces I could still see on the floor.

Rivers came down and already looked peeved about something as he thumbed through mail on his handheld device. "Junk, junk, junk…" He looked up and saw me out of place, not in my spot in front of the work baskets. "Why are you not working?"

"I was—" I was going to say 'picking up the pieces that Helga had dropped', but once again she was a traitorous little saving-her-own-neck slave.

"She's trying to hide the iron she dropped, Rivers!"

He looked at her and then down at my feet. His eyes popped up to mine and he looked absolutely murderous. But then he said softly, “I thought I told you not to call me that outside of the bedroom, baby doll.”

Yack, I just threw up in my mouth. I was the only slave he’d kept for so long. I didn’t know why. He always had two girls though, but the other one he rotated out every few months. It made no sense but I wasn’t allowed to ask. And I wasn’t allowed to call him Rivers to his face either. I called him Proprietor because that’s what he was. He was my owner and nothing else.

I looked over at his stupid, smug face. I’m sure the other girls ate up that expression. He was lean and kind of muscly. He always wore those stupid vintage, hip shirts. In the last few years, our planet had begun to adopt a few rare Earth-cultures with shirts having silly pictures on them and things like that. So brand names and objects that we no longer carried or used, they showcased on their clothes. Rivers was currently sporting a Google shirt. And he grated the nerves even further when he would say the logo name over and over when he thought no one was listening, because he was a big doofus. *“Google, google, google.”* His hair was blond with blue tips and he had tattoos on his hands. Snakes on each finger. I could only imagine the gross things he did and said, the puns alone…

Yeah. Yack.

I looked up to find him watching me. “What’s with the face?”

I grimaced harder. “I’m trying not to puke imagining someone who’ll have coitus with you.”

He raced across the room so fast I barely saw him move. He was wearing his hurtle boots, for people always running late and messengers. Or for jerkfaces who just wanted to be mean and scare people. They cost a pretty silver because they had to be connected to your cerebral or something. It skimmed you across the surface you were on, hovering just slightly. I didn’t know how it worked; I just knew that you thought it and it obeyed. And that Rivers had a pair.

He gripped my chin in his hard fingers, the snakes moved on his skin, hissing from the ends of his fingers and acting as though they'd bite me if they could only get to me. He always treated me like I was more than a slave, like I was *more* than just his property. I never understood it, but Rivers was a strange man. A strange proprietor. I'd stopped trying to understand him long ago.

"Watch your mouth, grub."

I felt my breath turn shallow. He only called me that when he was really pissed, when he was really trying to piss *me off.* Grub was the dirtiest word for a slave you could speak and he'd only ever called me that six times in the entire time that I'd been with him. Funny that every time had been instigated because of another one of his girls.

"Proprietor," I said carefully, "Helga is trying to use your balls to her advantage where she knows I have no pull. I have been in your ownership for ten years and have never lied to you. These girls are in and out every few months and apparently think that I'm their scapegoat every time they do something wrong, that you'll fall for it because you're having coitus with them. Please don't be that gullible guy."

"Who I have coitus with is not your business," he growled and flicked his eyes to her.

Helga was obviously getting the picture. The big picture. Ding, ding, ding, Helga!

"You mean you have coitus with all the other…slaves," she whispers, because saying that word aloud was a bit taboo, too. And Rivers having coitus with his slaves was just as bad as outright calling someone a grub, to polite society anyway. The lower level didn't care, but respectable men bought coitus the old-fashioned way instead of getting it for free from his slaves. What a tangled web we weave.

"Not me." I wrenched my face away from his hand. "Just get on with it. We both know that I wasn't the one who dropped the slivers of tin on the floor, we both know that you aren't going to punish her for it because you're sleeping with her, and we both know that you don't give a crap about any of it."

He stood straighter and lifted his chin. "I dislike it so much when your backbone starts showing. It just means that I have to beat it back down."

And right then I knew what I had to do. I didn't want to... I hoped my mother wasn't listening…

"You just go have dirty sex with your slaves and let me be—"

The slap across my face hurt, but him grabbing my hair hurt worse. I heard the alarm go off and the scanner's red laser light tried to scan me but couldn't find my face, so Rivers leaned back, still holding my hair, let it scan me, and then slammed my body against the wall as the speaker blared, telling me about my fine.

"Not only did you just cost me money, but I will not allow filth talk like that in my place and presence, do you understand me, grub? Your dead mother would be ashamed of you."

He was probably right, but I was getting out of here tonight so I hoped she would forgive me.

He took me over to the list on the wall, the list the Militia put on all the walls, of unacceptable words and behaviors. Among the list of words were sex and hate. Tons of emotional expressions, racial terms, any type of curse words or slang for it we weren't allowed to utter, even in the privacy of our homes, or the sensors and scanners would pick up on it and we would be fined. Everyone had to speak the same language. English. When the world leaders came together and made Congress, they decided that English was the most widely known language and it was the only language spoken, the only language allowed.

"Look at this list and know that it's here to help us, to keep us from going back to where we were. It's here to—"

"It's a world with no freedom. It's here for people like you, people at the top of the food chain," I groaned against his hold. "In a real world, the word *slave* would be up there, the word *grub* would be up there. In a real world, you wouldn't be about to take me for a beating that I didn't deserve because a girl that you're having coitus with dropped your tin shavings and blamed me."

He jerked me from the wall without a word and took me upstairs to his shop. I looked around at the people who were shopping, all knowing by the way he was holding me what was about to happen. It wasn't my first beating, but it would be my last. Those ropes, as they tied around my wrist, felt like the most freedom I'd had in the last ten years of my life. He looked down at me with a sadness that I wasn't sure was real or not as he took his belt from his pants. It was such an *Earth* thing, he had always told me. He read in our history books that the old slave-owners on Earth used to beat their slaves and children with their belts. So he wore one just in case he ever needed it, even though our pants were fitted to us biometrically. He moved around to my back. I waited, knowing this was what had to happen for my freedom.

I gripped that pole in the middle of the shop. The shoppers who had stopped looking for random metal items had stopped to watch—to watch the slave get hers, get what she deserved, because why else would her proprietor beat her?

When the first lash of metal and leather hit across my back, I gritted my teeth and told myself not to cry out, that this was what I needed to do to leave him forever, this was what my mother would want, that I was about to be reunited with her and my father, in my own way.

The second one hit and I hissed, couldn't be helped. He always used the end of the belt with the metal latch, so it bit into your flesh with every lash. I saw a man sneer in the back of the small crowd that had gathered to watch me take my licks. It wasn't the first time I'd been watched get a beating, people were fascinated by it, but the sickos that acted like I deserved it?

The third lash hit and I couldn't stop the small moan of pain that escaped. Rivers pressed his mouth to my ear from behind. "There's a crowd. Denying me the painful moans won't do you any good. I'll keep at it until you give in. I won't be embarrassed.

Just give it to me and I'll make it quick. Cry and I'll even give you the salve."

I gasped. He'd never given me the salve in all my time with him. The salve could practically numb you, and by the next day, you'd think you hadn't been beaten at all. It was a miracle salve. Why was he willing to give it to me?

I looked over my shoulder at him, saw nothing but ego. He wasn't trying to help me. He just wanted a good show. Well, this one time I was willing to give them one. Because I wanted to be done with this and go to the hole faster.

The next lash, I cried out harder. The last I cried actual tears and sobbed, letting the restraints on my wrists be the only thing holding me up. I let all my emotion bubble to the top for my mom and how I hated this man and this life and how I was so close to being done with it. The scream that erupted from me was primal and angry and sad and anguished. When I looked up, you would have thought they were watching their favorite play, they looked so enthralled.

"Is this what you want?" I rasped and jerked against my restraints. "Is this what you want to see? The slave beaten down and fighting for her life? The grub getting hers?"

Rivers looped his belt around his neck and roughly unclasped my hands as the onlookers watched me, saying nothing. He yanked me through to the side door, taking me to the back room, what Rivers called his 'dungeon', and tossed me unceremoniously inside.

"When will you learn that we all have our place, our parts to play?"

I scoffed, wincing as the slices on my back pulled. "When will you learn that it's up to you if you play those parts or not?"

He looked even more peeved, if that was possible, as he shut the door and locked it with the thumbprint scanner. I knew I wasn't getting any salve.

I moved swiftly, knowing that every second counted. I discounted the aching and hurting in my body. That didn't matter in the grand scheme of things right now. I had seven lashes total and that wasn't as bad as I could have gotten or had before. I'd gotten off lucky this time.

I moved swiftly, making sure the baggy of shavings was tucked securely in the bindings I'd tied around my breasts—since slaves didn't get fancy things like bras—before I began, and then I started to wiggle loose the old bars of the room he always made sure to leave me in. Every time he did, I made sure to work them until they came free, one at a time. It may have been one at a time, it may have been slow-going, it may have been agonizing waiting and biding my time, but this was the night.

Rivers would pay for keeping his old ways and not upgrading to a better system. Most of the windows and doors on buildings now were holographic projections and way more protective than an actual door would have been. But Rivers insisted that it was money wasted. And it was just another way for Congress to have a hold on you and keep tabs on you. True, Rivers, true. This once, though, your paranoia paid off for me. I wiggled the bars until each one let loose and gave way. I had been loosening them at my every visit to the *dungeon*, so they were already primed, it was just that last one. I spun it and shook it back and forth. Then I picked up one of the other bars and began to scrape away the concrete at the base of it. When the final bar came loose, I could have yelled to the stars. I grabbed the ledge of the high window and with shear will pulled myself up and into the window frame that I barely fit into.

I fell onto the street below it and gasped at the pain in my shoulder blade and back, but made myself get up and run to the end of the street. There was a ship in the dock there. I didn't know whose it was, but I could see the sign saying where it was going. And I was going to be on it.

I snuck on, tucked myself in a closet tightly, and prayed to my mother's God that no one would find me.

Chapter Two

ox·y·gen - a colorless, odorless reactive gas, the chemical element of atomic number eight and the life-supporting component of the air.

Maxton

"**R**eally?" he said smugly and looked at me with an air only an Elitist could pull off. "You really think I'm falling for that?"

I smirked my signature smirk and prayed to whoever was listening that this worked. "How can you not? Look at it." I held the silver ring in front of his face and painted the picture for him, just like I always did. "Picture it. You, her, out on Symphony Hill—"

"I'm taking her to Melody Ridge—"

"You're missing the point!" I yelled excitedly. "The point is that it doesn't matter where you give it to her, my man. The point is that it's her day of birth and you want her to remember this forever." I handed him some oxygen tabs. "You take these tabs."

He started to protest. "No, I couldn't."

"Is she worth it?"

"Of course!"

"Then you take the tabs!" I smiled, knowing I had him. "You can take the longer trip and not have to come back so soon. Rations, smations." I waggled an eye brow. "You get what I'm saying, my man? You take her out on the ridge, and you tell your grandkids one day that good ol' Maxton set it all up for you."

He let a breath go and smiled. Checkmate. "Wow. You're really doing me a solid, man."

"Nah," I assured him, "Because you're going to do me a solid in return, right?"

He gave me a sly grin. "Whatcha need?"

"Well, my boss told me I have to sell all these oxygen and gravity tabs by the end of the week. Think you can help me out? Know anybody?"

"Oh, yeah! I got you covered, man! I got buddies from school who never finished who are looking for tablets all the time." His look turned somber. Jackpot. "I mean, they're stand-up guys, they just hit a run of bad luck. You're all right helping my buddies, right?"

"Well," I muttered and shuffled my feet for good measure, "I don't know. I know it's illegal to sell to people without a diploma." I mean, not like what we're doing right now or anything…

"Man, I wouldn't ask, but you said you needed to get rid of it. We'll both be helping each other out." I hissed through my teeth. He watched. "Come on, man."

"All right. You got a deal. But I need all the money for the tablets up front."

"I'll get it all worked out. Thanks, man. Any way you're looking for a constant buyer? I'm sure they would be more than willing to be set up for something like that."

Bingo.

I smiled. "I think we can work something out."

He pulled out his handheld and worked out the deal right in front of me, just the way I liked it. I sold him the ring, met his buddies, gave them the goods, worked out the next shipment, and was back at the ship within an hour. I pulled my bed out of the wall and crashed onto it. I was as beat as I could remember being.

My boss, Havard, was working me like I imagined proprietors worked the slaves. But I wasn't a slave. He needed to back off. I earned my keep.

I laid my forehead against the pillow and sighed just as a bang resounded in the closet outside my room. This was a small ship, compared to other ships. If someone was going to hide, there weren't too many places to. I sighed, pissed and ticked off that my opportunity for sleep had been interrupted. Havard used to provide sleep induction for us, but once the Elites caught on—like they do everything—it became so expensive that he said we had to catch zzz's the old-fashioned way. But it made for a long night and frankly wasted time when, with sleep induction, I could get the sleep needed in half the time, no tossing and turning, no waiting to fall out, just conk—you're gone.

I scurried quietly over, yanking the double doors open to reveal…a girl.

No—a slave.

I could tell she was a slave because she was so thin. And she'd been beaten; I could tell from the blood on the back of her shirt. All my protective instincts rushed to the surface all at once, though I didn't know why. She was a slave, she obviously belonged to someone, but she was so…freaking striking. All that red hair, gray eyes, white skin and—

Maxton, stop.

"What are you doing here?" was the only thing my mouth could produce, gruffly.

"I…" she tried. She'd been crying. "I thought the ship was leaving in the morning. I didn't think I'd see anyone until it was already—"

"The ship does leave in the morning."

She gulped. "I know it's a lot to ask, but please, just don't say anything until we're already out to space at least." Her eyes begged. "Please."

"You're running away from your proprietor." Her eyes said 'yes', but she stayed silent. "That's a felony. You'll go to confinement for that."

"Hence the not telling anyone until we're out to space." She shook her head, her eyes going cold and hard. "Ten years is long enough. I think my debt is paid."

I almost gasped. Almost. Ten years. This girl was seventeen, eighteen maybe, nineteen at the most. She'd spent the majority of her life as a slave. I couldn't imagine it. I kept my face passive. "Come back to my room before someone sees you. You can stay there until we dock in Zone 8 tomorrow. Then you can be on your way."

I'd never seen someone look at me with such gratitude before, but I did work on the black market. I didn't have much time or opportunity for girls. This one had red hair that was long and a little curly, a little wild maybe, a thin body that indicated she didn't get to indulge on this planet, her head came to my nose, her gray eyes were wide and searching me, her skin was pale and gulp-inducing to look at it. So I tried not to look.

"Thank you."

I nodded. I told her to stay and knew she would. I went and got some dinner for us both, which was interesting. I told the cook I was really hungry because Havard had worked me too hard that day and I had skipped lunch. He must have bought it.

When I brought the food back and laid it out on my bed, the girl acted like it was foreign to her, like she'd never seen it before.

I chuckled. "Have you never seen a piece of bacon?"

"No," she whispered. "What is it?"

"Are you serious?"

"Very."

I looked at her as she looked at the meat. "Try it." Her eyes ticked up to mine. "Go on." She picked up the bacon first and took a bite so tentative it was pathetic. But she moaned and that moan caused me to gulp as it rippled through my body. She looked at the other food on the plate and then up at me.

"What's this?"

"You've never had pancakes before either?"

"All I've ever had was bread and vegetables. Green beans mostly."

I grimaced. She was from the stacks. "Really?" She didn't answer. Must have known it was rhetorical. "It's the most delicious thing on that plate. Eat up. I can't wait to watch you take a bite." I grinned.

But she wasn't worried about me a lick. She ate that whole plate like it was her last meal, or her first, depending on how you looked at it, softly moaning and groaning the entire time. She licked the syrup off her thumb when she was done and I wondered for a second if she was a spy. Had Havard sent her here to see if I'd let a stowaway stay?

I watched her and knew that wasn't true when she turned with the plate, looking for a proper place to set it...like a *good little slave*. The blood on the back of her shirt was a reminder to me that this wasn't some game, and she wasn't just some girl.

She was a convict now, no matter how much I wanted to deny it.

End of Preview

Find information about this book and all of Shelly's books at her website and social medias below. Shelly's books are available on all sites, wherever books are sold.

www.shellycraneauthor.com

41809135R00063

Printed in Poland
by Amazon Fulfillment
Poland Sp. z o.o., Wrocław